Poetry Adventure and Love

Ed Elgar

Copyright © 2015 Ed Elgar

All rights reserved.

ISBN:1523368101
ISBN-13: 978-1523368105

Author's Note

This is a work of fiction. The names, characters, businesses, places, events, incidents and dialogues, are either the products of the author's imagination or used in a fictitious manner. Any resemblance to actual persons, living or dead, or actual events is purely coincidental.

The Yolngu aboriginal people in Arnhem Land, in the remote far north of Australia, are quite real, although the community of Umbakala is quite fictitious. The village, the people and some of the events mirror the reality of these communities today. English is a sixth language for the native Yolngu people who live there, and even today, they sing, dance and practice their ancient ceremonies. If you dare to travel to this part of the world, you will need a permit to visit Yolngu country and once inside, you will find a number of art centres which promote and sell Yolngu art and culture.

The Garma Festival which is also featured in this novel is also a very real annual event. Visitors from all over the world travel to Arnhem land to witness this beautiful celebration of Yolngu art, music, dance and culture.

CONTENTS

	Map of Arnhem Land	i
	The Garma Festival	ii
1	Arnhem Land	Pg 1
2	Umbakala	Pg 12
3	Sir Galahad	Pg 22
4	The Poem	Pg 34
5	Meeting Dumatja Again	Pg 45
6	Yolngu Barbeque	Pg 55
7	Yolngu Church	Pg 66
8	The Axe and the Art Centre	Pg 77
9	The Curse	Pg 88
10	The Yacht Race	Pg 98
11	Garma Festival	Pg 108
12	Crocodile Creek	Pg 118

Map of Arnhem Land

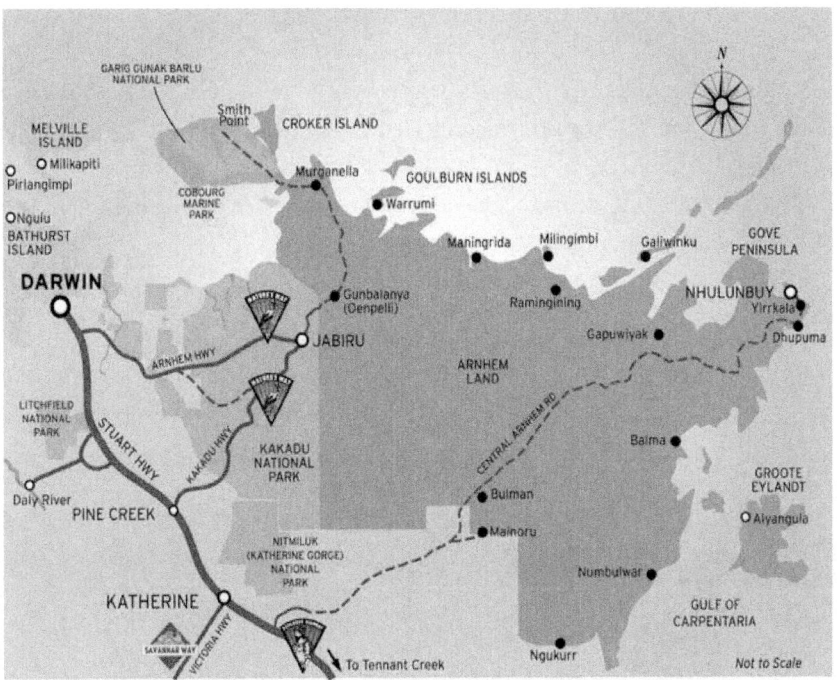

Arnhem land is in the far north of tropical Australia and is on the north east tip of the Northern territory. The only road in to Nhulunbuy, is generally only accessible 6 months of the year due to swollen, crocodile infested rivers.

The Garma Festival

Garma, the largest and most vibrant annual celebration of Yolngu (Aboriginal people of north east Arnhem Land) culture.

Garma incorporates visual art, ancient storytelling, dance and music, as well as other important forums. This annual festival is held at the Gulkula ceremonial grounds in northeast Arnhem Land, near the town of Nhulunbuy. People travel from all over the world to visit this exciting spectacle.

Although some of the scenes in this book are set at Garma, the action of course, is entirely fictitious.

1 Arnhem Land

Cassie sprung up in her bunk and rubbed her eyes. A thin beam of moonlight appeared to be sawing its way into the boat, as Serendipity rocked sideways. *Where am I?* Something was wrong. The sounds were wrong; the movement was wrong. There was no longer the regular up and down motion over the swell or the gentle slap of the bow waves. Cassie jumped to her feet and was thrown from side to side as she stumbled through the cabin in her sun-bleached T-shirt. She winced as she banged her leg on the map table. Then she heard the flapping of sails and the whine of the autopilot motor complaining. Something was *very* wrong.

By the time Cassie had flung on the life vest and turned on the deck lights, she was fully awake, alone, on the Arafura Sea. Through the blackness, she could see a faint light on the horizon. *That must be Nhulunbuy,* she thought, *finally, after three months.* Out in the cockpit, Cassie grabbed the helm and turned the wheel to starboard. No response! The wheel spun freely in her hands, brown and calloused from thousands of miles of tugging on ropes and winding winches. The usual resistance as the wheel turned the rudder, was gone. She remembered the noise that woke her. Fear was driving her now. Without conscious thought, she ran down below to check the bilges – relief – no water coming in. Cassie knew then, she'd probably collided with a shipping container. Her dad had warned her about the dangers,

"Keep a look-out for containers Cass, sea's full of them. Sometimes they'll be floating just under the surface – damn menace!"
It was three months since she saw her dad. Three months since she'd sailed under the Golden Gate, three months without a hitch – and now this.

As she furled the jib and lowered the mainsail, the knot untangled in her stomach, but the fear was now replaced with an aching loneliness. She thought of James. *Ten years – why didn't I leave him sooner?* As Cassie settled in to wait for dawn, she remembered the time James had become angry when after a long day at the beach, she climbed into his precious sports car with a little sand on her feet. She smiled at the memory, wondering what he'd think of the bits of sand and sea weed stuck to the floor of the cock-pit. Content that there was no immediate danger of leaks, she hugged her knees tightly to her chest, staring into the blackness. What would she find in this untamed place they call Arnhem Land? Before she left San Francisco, Cassie had researched the area and learnt about the Yolngu people – the aboriginal tribes who lived in the vast tropical north of Australia and typically spoke 6 languages, including English. Just as well as English was her only language! She knew there were tropical cyclones and that Nhulunbuy, the only town for hundreds of miles had no road access for most of the year. What if the people here didn't like her – didn't like her ideas? Would she be accepted as an American in this remote aboriginal community? Would she be accepted as a woman in a patriarchal society?

As Serendipity rocked in the swell, Cassie's body swayed in time with the waves, in rhythm with her breathing. There was an occasional scent of eucalypt, mingled with the fresh warm salty air of the tropics. A lanyard started tinkling annoyingly on the mast like a tympani in tune with Serendipity's swaying. She couldn't be bothered going forward to stop the noise and snuggled further into the corner of the cockpit, tucking her legs to one side and folding her arms which had sprouted unexpected goose bumps. Cassie's mind drifted into her future uncertainties. She remembered the pictures she had downloaded of black skinned dancers, bodies painted with ochre, their steps throwing up dust and the didgeridoo players sitting in the sand. Her moist eyes widened in anticipation and her heart began to drum the beat of the Yolngu tribes.

When the sun was fully bright, Cassie took off her weathered shorts and t-shirt, donned her diving mask, snorkel and flippers, tethered herself to her beloved Serendipity, and slipped overboard. The water was like a cosy bath, slipping soothingly over her nut-brown skin. It was so clear, the water, the sky; for an instant she almost forgot why she was in this azure paradise. Holding her breath she dived down, kicking her legs with smooth long strokes. As her ears popped with the depth, Cassie could see that the rudder had been snapped off completely. Gone. A gouge in the hull first sent shivers, then a wave of relief for having bought an old fibreglass boat. The hull was much thicker in the early days of fibreglass.

"So much better than these new Tupperware things." her dad had said when they had first inspected Serendipity.
Cassie resurfaced and went straight back down again, she began to enjoy this excuse to be in the water. Running her hands along the rut in the hull, she felt along the bristling glass fibres with her fingers, searching for any holes or cracks. Finding no holes was liberating, so Cassie pushed herself

along the hull to the bow, occasionally looking around to see if there were any sharks or other sea creatures out there. She had seen another pod of dolphins yesterday, a couple of them had surfed the bow waves. She had run up to the bow and talked to them, her favourite animal. *Nothing to see today,* she thought; then began almost reluctantly to swim back to the rear of the boat. Floating on her back toward the stern ladder, Cassie lazed and stretched, allowing the water to make its final soothing caresses, before hauling herself back into the cockpit. Taking off the dive gear, Cassie allowed herself the luxury of air-drying her naked body on the open deck for a few minutes. Then popping on the coffee pot, she poured out her usual muesli and milk while she lingered in the sun's warming rays, planning her emergency repairs.

It took Cassie only two hours to dismantle her dining table, drill a few well-placed holes and lash the makeshift teak rudder to the stern. *Not perfect,* she thought, but it would do the job – only a few more hours and she would be in Gove Harbour and besides, she knew how to steer using only the sails. Cassie felt strong and confident again as she stretched her legs across the cockpit and rested her tired arms like she would on the back of her sofa back home. Yet, this was now her home; all she had was on board the boat, her past life was floating away across the world. Every so often she thrilled at the excitement and laughed at her newfound freedom. Her only doubt now rested in thoughts about her new job in Umbakala. Sometimes she felt like a fraud; felt that everyone around her was more capable, more certain. Like she had on her first sailing race when she was six years old. She came last that time, but her dad was so happy afterwards. He picked her up, hugged her and then they went out for ice cream to celebrate. Cassie hated losing, but the memory made her a little sad. She missed her dad, but she hardly ever thought about James any more. When she did, Cassie was happy that there were less and less thoughts about this part of her past life. Over the last few months her mistakes had been swept away with salty water, not salty tears.

Ben watched as Garrawarra locked the tool shed behind them with a sturdy chain.

"See you tomorrow Garrawarra. We'll finish setting up the reinforcing in the foundations so we can pour the concrete for Alanja's house next week."

"No worries Ben, the boys are keen 'bout this building' stuff. Their grandfathers did it – reckon they can do it too," said Garrawarra, teeth glistening in a broad smile. He added, "You stay out in the sun this long Boss and soon you be black as me!"

Ben laughed and clutched his foreman's shoulder as they turned to head for their respective homes. As Ben made his way down the hill toward the bay, he glanced back to see Garrawarra striding towards his home through the litter of coke cans and take-away containers. Ben still found it hard to come to terms with how a thousand people living in this community could live with all the litter. In the month that he'd been at Umbakala, he was slowly unravelling some of the mysteries of the Yolngu culture. He knew from reading a couple of anthropology books and talking to some of the elders that the Yolngu were once a proud warrior race who lived as one with the land and sea. *The dancing, the songs, the didgeridoo are still here*, he mused, *but only just*.

Ben walked down the winding path, past the art centre perched on the cliff, to the jetty and small boat yard. He suddenly spotted a sail boat coming into the bay. *Another world traveller*, he thought. Gove harbour was an almost essential stop for the adventurous circumnavigators. As he approached the boatyard, he could see Mario's tanned muscles straining as he scraped the barnacles off one of the wealthy miner's catamarans. Ben gave him a wave and a smile as he passed, but thought it best not to interrupt him while he was working. He knew that Mario loved to have a beer and a chat in between jobs. Besides, he was tired. Even though Ben's job description was to train the aboriginal building team, he led by example and dug the trenches side by side with the Yolngu men. This way he knew he was quickly able to build their respect and besides he wasn't one for just standing around when there was a job to be done.

Ben jumped aboard his late model sail boat, eager to complete his last routine maintenance job before the sun went down. He had decided to treat himself when he sold his half share in the Sydney building business to his partner. After buying an investment apartment at the Gold Coast and some shares, there was still enough money left over for this little beauty. As he started pulling apart the winch to re-grease it, he proudly admired her shiny hull and sleek fast lines. Down south, Ben would have had only a glass or two of wine with dinner, but here in the tropics, the first gulp of cold beer at the end of a sweaty day seemed almost essential, just to cool down. He opened the tinny as he sat in the cockpit with his back to the setting sun, oblivious to the new arrival heading toward the jetty.

Cassie could see the other yacht tied to the jetty and the space behind – room enough for Serendipity. With time to spare, she deftly furled the sail and made to spin the boat by hauling on her makeshift rudder, a manoeuvre she had done countless times in her own marina back home. Cassie loosened one of the knots holding the rudder and started to apply pressure to slide her ten tonnes of ancient fibreglass precisely where she wanted. She hadn't noticed the chaffing on one of the ropes. As

Cassie pulled harder, the frayed rope snapped, sending her plummeting to the cockpit floor – she groaned with pain as her thigh was punched by a blunt steel latch. Ben turned abruptly when he heard the flap of a sail. His eyes and mouth widened as he saw an apparently unmanned boat aiming its anchor straight at his hull. The crash sent him tumbling, bits of winch springs washing with beer and grease in his cockpit.

Cassie meanwhile was disbelieving as she lay sprawled face down on the deck. Spots of blood appeared on her shirt as she felt a warm trickle from her nose. Her first thought was to secure the boat to the jetty as she limped to the rail and cast off the first mooring rope. Ben was already on the jetty.

"What do you think you're playing at lady? You've smashed my boat," he cried, incredulous. "Well? What were you thinking? You had heaps of jetty to aim at, why did you have to hit my boat?"

Cassie stood transfixed as Ben tied off both mooring ropes like a snake on the prowl. Her body began shaking – tears began to stream down her cheek and she found herself sobbing involuntarily, but desperately not wanting to.

"I ... I'm sorry," Cassie blubbered. "I've lost my rudder – I've got no control!" she pleaded tearfully.

"I'll say you haven't," rattled Ben, a little bit more subdued, but the veins in his neck still pulsing with fury.

Cassie stared at this man, her body shaking – she couldn't stop the sobs or the quivers. She saw Ben suddenly stop and stare at the blood on her shirt. He had barely got out the words,

"Are you alright ...", when she looked around toward the sound of footsteps running down the jetty. Another man leapt aboard Serendipity. This was almost too much for Cassie, her head was pounding, her nose and leg were numb with pain and these two strangers surrounded her. Hardly the arrival she had expected.

"Come on," Mario said gently as he put an arm around her shoulders and guided her forearm with the other. "I think you should sit down lady – Ben have you got some tissues handy?"

Cassie felt a surge of relief and pleasure as Mario's strong arms supported her. She hadn't been touched for a long time. She looked into his Mediterranean eyes and found a smile.

"Thank you. I'm sorry for causing such a fuss. I really thought I had it under control – you see my rudder broke last night and I fixed up this makeshift rudder and it was working well ... until ..." Her words faded as Ben arrived with a tissue box and clean white handkerchief.

"So why didn't you just anchor in the bay or call out for help?" said Ben unkindly.

"Let it go Ben," Mario warned him.

Cassie sensed the testosterone rising as she started to regain her self-control.

"Look, I'm okay guys, let's just calm down and talk this through."

"So who's going to pay for the damage to my boat? She's nearly new you know." Ben's tone was now lower and steelier.

"Come on Ben, not now mate; let's see to the lady first."

"You seem to be doing quite well without me," snarled Ben as he jumped onto the deck and clambered back onto his own boat to clean up the mess and examine the damage.

"Don't worry about Ben, he's okay really." said Mario as he dabbed Cassie's face tenderly with the handkerchief. She recoiled slightly with the pain, but was also weakened by the sight of Mario's rippling forearms and powerful chest at such close proximity.

Her next memory was waking up in a strange bed with a splitting dull ache behind her eyes. She could smell a strange mix of liniment and incense as she tried to sit up.

"Don't get up – just have this." She felt a strong hand against her shoulder blades and a cup of warm sweet liquid pressed to her lips.

"What is it?" groaned Cassie.

"It's just a sweet herbal tea my Grandma used to make. You fainted out there on your boat – I wasn't sure if you needed a doctor or what." Mario smiled then brushed Cassie's dark wavy hair from her face. Cassie felt the tickles as the tips brushed over her bare shoulders. His eyes moved from her shoulders to her eyes - she could see his pupils, large dark spheres demanding attention from her.

"You're very beautiful, you know," his white teeth beamed with confidence. "What's your name, beautiful lady?"

"Cassie." she smiled half-heartedly, uncertain if this was a white knight or a gigolo. She had never experienced attention like this from a man before. Were all Australian men this forward? "I'll bet you say that to all the girls."

"Only the *really* beautiful ones," he replied, smirking. "Let's see, the last time I said that was – eight years ago." Mario looked off into the distance, his cheeky grin fading, as he casually put his hand on top of hers. Cassie instinctively pulled her hand away, even though she felt a tingling through her body that hadn't happened in years, since she first went out with James.

"Eight years is a long time. Does this mean there aren't *any* women up in these parts? There must be a good story there somewhere?" remarked Cassie, her head beginning to clear and she became more confident at handling this man's attentions.

"Yeah there is but none *that* beautiful. I said it on my honeymoon." Again he grinned like a small naughty boy who had been caught with his hand in the lolly jar.

"Well Mario, I hope you don't get any ideas and imagine then and now are like .... the same thing!" Cassie purred, starting to enjoy this game.

"They could be the same," said Mario, as he dropped on one knee beside the bunk in his boathouse bedroom. "I could marry a girl like you, beautiful *and* you have a boat!"

"Ah, an ulterior motive, you're really after my boat, aren't you?"

"Okay, you're onto me. You American women are so switched on."

"You Australian men are so full of it! By the way, what do you do here and who was that other guy, the one whose boat I smashed up ... and .... where am I .... how did I get here?"

"Boy, you know how to change a subject. Okay, I run this little boat yard. The Yolngu and I have this arrangement and I pay them rent for the land. My dad started it off in the '60's, he's dead now, but I grew up here. The other bloke? That's Ben. He and I carried you to my place after you fainted. Ben's only been here a month, he's come in to train the local building team. About time too, they been havin' houses put up by white contractors for the last thirty years. Look it's gone dark already, what about some tucker Cassie? Are you hungry? I don't suppose you're up for cooking tonight."

"Ravenous, but I couldn't eat another fish just now. I've been eating them for the past four months."

"How about some bangers and mash then?"

"What?"

"Oh sorry, I forgot you were a yank." Mario laughed as he walked backwards across the dimly lit room toward a bulky chest freezer that stood in the corner, next to a sink and stained kitchen cupboards.

"Sausages and mashed potatoes, smothered in tomato sauce, er, I mean ketchup!"

"That sounds fine, thanks. Could I have a glass of water please?" Cassie made to rise up, but felt giddy again. "Sorry," she said, "I'm not usually this useless."

"No worries mate," Mario handed Cassie a smudged jam jar filled to the brim with water. The jar seemed to epitomise the messy room, the dust on the window sill, the empty bread wrapper on the floor. It did not look to Cassie as if Mario had ever had a woman in his life. He quickly dashed back to the stove and lit the gas, then flung four solid frozen sausages onto a fry pan. "Now it's your turn," Mario said with his back to Cassie, as he started cutting onions and peeling potatoes in a grimy steel sink.

"What?"

"What are you doing here? Who are you?"

Before Cassie could answer, there was a knock on the door and Ben barged in. He saw Cassie propped up on Mario's bed with a drink and smelled the onions frying on the stove.

"I just came to say, I've tied down your boat properly with springers. We've got big tides here you know."

"Right Ben," volunteered Mario. "Everything's okay here mate, I'm just making some dinner for Cassie. She was just about to tell us what she's doing in Umbakala."

"Right then I'll leave you to it," said Ben tersely. "We can talk about the damage to my boat tomorrow." Ben turned quickly as he uttered his last words and left the door banging behind him.

"Is he always this uptight?" asked Cassie, as the image of Ben's powerful legs silhouetted by the sunset lingered. She liked nicely shaped men's legs and had often wandered if it was normal. Wasn't it men who were tits, bums and legs fanciers? She cast an eye to the sink and noticed that Mario's legs were a bit bowed, strong, tanned and manly; nothing like James's pale wiry legs. She was still daydreaming when Mario answered.

"No he's alright, I think he's just had a blue today with Mike Britliff, the community CEO."

"Mike? He's the one that offered me the job."

"What job? You don't mean the art centre job?"

"That's right," said Cassie, looking down at her blood stained sweaty t-shirt. All of a sudden she felt unfeminine and ugly and desperately yearned for a shower.

"Mario, I'd kill for a shower and change of clothes"

"No problem, see that wardrobe in the corner? My ex-wife left some of her stuff there; she must have been about your size. Help yourself. Not doing me any good. The bathroom's just through there." He pointed with a sharp knife in between cutting up more potatoes.

Feeling pressure of the dried blood in her nostrils, Cassie limped across to the wardrobe, suddenly aware of the ache from the bruise on her thigh. A musky smell lingered in the cupboard, mixed with the last gasp of rose scented pot pourri. She flicked through the colourful slinky dresses, thinking how odd that a woman would have need of such clothes in this wild isolated place. Cassie chose a pale yellow cotton dress that enhanced the deep glow of her tanned legs and found a new looking pair of undies in a drawer. There were some bras there too, but she decided to go bra-less; it was too hot. *If Mario gets excited, that's his problem*, she thought.

The shower was faded chrome with copper green stains which matched the ancient green porcelain toilet and basin. Cassie's feet slipped slightly on the worn concrete floor. There were no tiles and just a brittle plastic shower curtain, patterned with mould. It reminded her of the yacht club bathroom in Fiji. She'd expected better in a first world country, but when the luxury of the hot water flowed down her face for the first time in weeks, Cassie surrendered her nakedness to the flow as the rivulets massaged curves and washed away the weariness of travel and the pains from her fall. On Serendipity, bathing was done with a bucket of tepid sea water from over the side. She had become comfortable with her nakedness in the middle of the Pacific, but still had pale untanned breasts and hips. Cassie thought about her teacher colleagues back in the States and how jealous they would be of her bronzed skin – but maybe not so envious of this third world bathroom. She hoped that the house that came with the art centre manager's job would be a lot nicer than this.

"Ave you washed away down the drain hole luv?" Mario shouted through the corrugated tin door. Cassie's eyes went to the bolt she had carefully shut after entering the bathroom. Her arms instinctively crossed over her breasts in a moment of uncertainty. She was naturally modest and a slight surge of panic rose to her flushed face. Cassie was determined not to get the wrong kind of reputation in Umbakala and besides, Mario seemed nice but who knew if she could trust him?

"Dinner's about ready ..."

"Just give me a minute Mario, I'll be right out." Cassie quickly dried herself with a thin bristly towel and slipped on the light dress. *It's good to feel like a woman again*, thought Cassie, as she walked back into Mario's den.

"Whoop – wooo," Mario wolf whistled as he stared shamelessly at Cassie's bare legs. The flimsy dress was midway up her thighs. She turned her blushing cheeks away while placing her neatly folded dirty clothes on Mario's bunk.

"Mario," she said firmly. "Where I come from it's just dumb building workers and street cleaners who think a girl likes to be wolf whistled at."

"Really? Most Aussie girls don't seem to mind at all." He flashed a perfect set of white teeth in Cassie's direction.

"Listen, I just want to be sure you don't get the wrong idea about me. I'm not that kind of girl."

"Well then, we'd better find out what sort of girl you really are. Anyway – sit down, gorgeous and get it into ya!"

He placed two steaming plates piled high with fat sausages and a mountain of mashed potato. A bottle of tomato sauce was already in the middle of the wooden table with rings where coffee mugs had left their mark. Mario then ceremoniously placed a stubby of beer in front of Cassie and raised his own bottle.

"Salute! To amoré and beautiful women!"

Cassie had almost finished eating dinner while Mario was only half way through. He had been doing most of the talking. She found out that he had left Arnhem Land when he was nineteen and found work servicing luxury yachts in a marina in Brisbane. It was there that he had met his wife, who had a rich daddy and a large yacht. *That would explain the dresses*, thought Cassie.

"So how long have you been divorced?"

"Rhonda left two years ago. She just took off one day with a rich French yachtsman. I guess I wasn't good enough for her. Good riddance I say."

Cassie couldn't help wondering, from the tone of his voice, if under that bravado, Mario was still hurting. She reflected on how she might have felt if James had been unfaithful – but then she dismissed that possibility, he was too boring to have a fling with another woman.

Quite suddenly Cassie felt very tired. Today's adventures had been entirely unexpected, and subconsciously she was starting to let go. There was nothing left of the day but sleep.

"Mario, thank you for everything you've done. The meal was lovely but I need to get back to my boat now, I'm so tired."

Mario stood and saluted in mock fashion. "At your service mam! You've made my day. Hey, I was the first to have you – you'll have to watch out now when the miners hear there's a beautiful woman with a boat in town."

Cassie chose not to respond; she felt grateful for Mario's kindness and was somehow able to forgive his brazen behaviour. She suddenly shuddered with pleasure as Mario placed a large hand on the small of her back, almost half encircling her tiny waist.

"The dock light's on, but I'll come and walk you to your boat."

"No really, there's no need Mario, I just want to be on my own right now. I'll probably see you in the morning. I'll need some directions to the council office."

"I'm usually up at dawn," replied Mario, "start work early before it gets too hot. See you tomorrow beautiful." He leaned in to kiss Cassie, but was too late; she had already turned to leave, anticipating Mario's move.

"Suppose I'd better wash up the..." were his last words as he disappeared into his tin boatshed.

Cassie could hear the night voices of the frogs and smell the eucalypt of the Australian bush that surrounded the foreshore of the bay. She looked back up the hill to see lights scattered in the bush. Cassie had learnt a little about the Yolngu living in Umbakala and despite her fatigue became more awake with the excitement of being in this exotic place. From the bush she could hear an excited young man's voice, "Yo wawa ..." and distant girl's laughter. *Tomorrow was the start of her new life here,* she mused as she padded barefoot along the splintery hardwood docks of the dock. As she began to climb aboard Serendipity, Cassie was startled by the deep voice from the dark.

"I see you didn't waste any time then."
She clutched her laundry close to her chest and looked around. She saw Ben sitting in the moonlight on the prow of his boat.

"W-what do you mean by that?" trying valiantly to regain her composure.

"Looks like you've been shopping for clothes – don't know what you might have used for money though." There was a recognisable tone of sarcasm in his voice.

"What I do is none of your business, Ben, or whatever your name is. As far as I'm concerned after I arrange to have your boat fixed up, I don't want anything to do with you – you're rude, you're arrogant ..." she was unable to finish the sentence before Ben interjected,

"Suits me lady," as he bounded down into the darkness of his cabin.

Cassie's heart pounded with indignation as she stormed below decks, slipped off her newly acquired dress and crawled into her still, soft berth. It was only seconds before her anger and racing thoughts were overtaken by exhaustion. Cassie had barely covered her aching bare body with a sheet before she was fast asleep.

2   Umbakala

Cassie woke up suddenly and her first thought was how still everything was. She had woken up a few times in the night out of habit, but there were no sails to check and no need to navigate any more. A sinking feeling in her stomach came as she saw Ben's legs through a porthole. He was striding strongly along the jetty toward land. She rushed to the cockpit to get a better look, feeling a bit ashamed at her voyeurism. Cassie made an involuntary sigh as she eyed Ben's broad shoulders and sculptured thighs and calf muscles below the khaki work shorts. Quickly chastising herself, she rationalised. No, Ben might have a great body but he wasn't as handsome as Mario and besides he was not a very nice man. She resolved to have as little to do with him as possible.

Breakfast was her own concoction designed for weeks of sailing without refrigeration. Serendipity had an ice box for when she was in port but for now she poured out the raw oat muesli mixed with dry fruit and nuts then poured on the reconstituted powdered milk. Cassie yearned for the latté and croissant breakfasts she used to have at her favourite cafe before work, but decided this adventure was worth the sacrifice and besides she had never felt healthier in all her thirty one years.

By eight-thirty, Cassie had cleaned the galley and tidied up the boat. She put on a cotton sarong, a modest white blouse and a pair of new leather sandals. She had decided back in San Francisco this outfit would be suitable in the tropics for a professional. Even this early in the day, she felt a trickle of sweat run between her shoulder blades and a warm breeze wafted out of the gumtrees rustling her skirt. Cassie had already been told by Mike that for cultural and modesty reasons women had to wear long skirts. It was inappropriate to wear shorts or even jeans. There had been some suggestion in her research that legs were considered erotic by Yolngu men while breasts were not really an issue. She also remembered that making direct eye contact for long was considered disrespectful. Cassie tried to remember everything she had learnt, eager to fit into their culture and help the Yolngu develop their art centre.

As she stepped off the jetty she saw Mario hosing down the hull of a boat near to the path that headed up the hill towards where she'd seen the lights last night.

"G'day Cassie" beamed Mario as he looked Cassie up and down. "Wow, you look great! Did you sleep well?"

Cassie returned his smile with a slight blush. "Thanks Mario, I feel so much better today. Thanks for looking after me. That shower and a good sleep did the trick."

"What about the bangers and mash?"

"Oops, forgot about that. Yup, they were good too. I'll have to make dinner for you soon to say thank you when I get settled."

"That would be great. Do you want me to take you up to the council office to meet Mike?"

"That's okay Mario, I'm happy to find my own way if you could just give me some directions."

Cassie could see Mario was busy. That gave him another tick in her man assessment box. Hard worker, as well as handsome, nice smile and easily tannable skin. She cleared her mind of these thoughts as she wound up the path through the gum trees. Cassie came across a dirt road and in the distance on the left she saw a building with peeling white paint and a dull green tin roof. She could just make out the sign on the outside, 'Umbakala Art Centre'. Her step quickened with excitement, the dull ache in her sore thigh was now forgotten. She already imagined a fresh coat of white paint on the walls and a new ochre roof and palm trees in the grassy patch on the cliff top.

She hadn't gone much further when she came upon two outsized steel sheds, surrounded by a barbed wire security fence. There were about ten black men in faded orange shirts and khaki shorts like Ben had been wearing. The sun glistened on their moist skin as the tallest of the men smiled from a distance and shouted out to her, "Hello, yapa."

Cassie waved back demurely and said hi, thinking, *Well, that's two out of three friendly men so far.* She quietly hoped that the women would be more friendly and easy to engage. Cassie knew she had a lot to learn. She had only been a high school art teacher for eight years after leaving college but then her parents had been in business. She had spent holidays learning how to sell antiques and furniture in the family shop. *Selling art should be much the same,* she thought, although she couldn't help but hold on to a nagging uncertainty.

Soon she was on the edge of town. The dusty dirt road she was on began to criss-cross others. There were houses amongst the gum trees and an occasional giant rain tree. She had read that the Macassans from

Indonesia in the North used to trade with the Yolngu and were responsible for planting the seeds of these magnificent trees. She saw a group of small children in brightly coloured clothing playing in the dirt with a mangy dog, tufts of hair hanging from its blistered skin. They were beside a corrugated steel house with broken windows. An old man sat in the shadows of the verandah staring blankly straight ahead. A woman with a mass of black curly hair and a long frayed dress came toward Cassie along the road. She was carrying a naked black baby in one arm and a plastic shopping bag in the other. She smiled warmly at Cassie, "Hello yapa", as she walked past. Cassie returned the greeting then looked beyond some dusty homes to a sizeable building with a sign on the almost derelict wire fence, with crooked posts and rusty steel strands. 'Umbakala Council', it read under the layer of orange dust.

As Cassie walked up the concrete path to the entrance, a light breeze wafted through her skirt cooling the perspiration beads clinging to her body. No one was near the council building but in the distance, Yolngu in colourful shirts and long flowing dresses were walking in all directions to and from what looked like the general store. Cassie made a mental note to get some Australian dollars and buy some much needed fresh food. She was desperate for fresh fruit and vegetables after weeks of dried beans and tinned food.

The security doors were locked and instead of a keyhole a security keypad loomed. Cassie knocked as she pondered the paradox of a modern security device in an almost stone age environment. There had to be someone inside, there was a shiny cherry red Landcruiser parked out the front. While she patiently waited, two white troop carriers drove past slowly, each filled with black faces. There was a constant sound of distant voices in a strange language. The nasal tone and sounds were unfamiliar to her. Her European back-packing trip with her best friend after college hadn't prepared Cassie for a culture such as this.

Just then Cassie turned, startled to see a Yolngu man with a wad of curly black hair speckled with strands of grey. A stale sweat smell drifted from his orange t-shirt and dusty grey shorts. He made no eye contact as he reached past Cassie and fingered the keypad.

"You lookin' for someone yapa?"
Cassie's stomach was knotted now. She didn't want it to be, but all of a sudden it felt like her first day at school and she had just seen the bogey man at the same time.

"Y- yes." Cassie stammered, her mouth dry. "I'm the new art centre manager, I'm here to see Mike Britliff."

"Oh, yo" he almost shouted, revealing a set of perfect white teeth and a warm smile. "Come in, Mike should be here already. He car out the front," he gestured toward the red car. He finally made eye contact and extended a sinewy hand to Cassie. Cassie smiled back uncertainly, but was secretly relieved that this man was friendly.

"I'm the shire president," he announced. "My name Alanja, Charlie Alanja. We been waitin' for you to come. Art Centre been needin' someone to kick 'im in pants for a while now!" He laughed and coughed a smoker's cough, as Cassie entered an open office, papers and files sitting in apparent disarray on a number of desks. The floor had streaks as if a mop had dampened the dust and caked it in swirls but the air conditioning was cool and welcoming as Cassie followed Alanja down a dark corridor past a row of offices.

"Mike, someone 'ere to see you. New art centre manager," chuckled Alanja as he indicated for Cassie to go into the office.

"Thank you Charlie," came the high pitched voice from the round ruddy face. "Welcome to Umbakala Miss Greenway." He motioned for her to sit. "We didn't know when you'd be arriving; we've never had an art centre manager sail half way round the world to get here."
Cassie took his hand before sitting down. It felt soft and damp like a skinned mullet.

"Please, Cassie – can I call you Mike or would you prefer Mr Britliff?"

"No, no, we're not too formal around here" he said, but was betrayed by his freshly ironed white cotton shirt, buttons stretched by his belly, dark blue silk tie badly tied at the neck and wet stains under his armpits.
Cassie sat quietly as Mike talked, almost non-stop, for the next hour. She could hear noises in the hallway and other offices as people started coming into the building. She could hear Yolngu spoken and English in Australian and Yolngu accents. There was occasional laughter contrasting with Mike's serious dissertation on the council, Yolngu people and art centre matters. The more he spoke, the more oily he sounded to Cassie. She wasn't able to figure why, and very much wanted not to have these feelings that she could not trust this man. She wondered if her intuition could be wrong about both Ben and Mike.

"That's about as much as I can tell you for the moment Cassie. I'm sure you'll be able to deal with the poor financial situation, Council will do everything we can to help you. Just remember, the pressure's on for you to sell as much artwork as you can, as quickly as you can." Mike stood up, a thin smile on his narrow lips as he rubbed his hands together vigorously. "Come and I'll introduce you to the other staff, then we'll have some morning tea in the board room to celebrate your arrival. Then I'll show you round town and take you to the art centre so you can get started. No rest for the wicked, eh?"
Cassie shivered as she stood up, not sure if it was the air conditioning or

Mike that brought on the goose bumps.

Later as Mike drove her around, Cassie memorised the locations of the store, the three take away shops, the medical centre, school and various little government offices, many of them temporary demountable buildings, which had stayed beyond their intended date. All the streets were dusty dirt with pot holes, discarded take away containers and soft drink cans flattened by the steady procession of white four wheel drives. The houses were scattered over a large area and were separated by stunted but straight limbed gum trees. The women all wore brightly coloured dresses and most seemed to Cassie to be carrying babies or toddlers. The airport was a dirt strip where ten seater airbuses came and went daily, ferrying people to distant communities. Cassie had already learnt how Yolngu had a complex web of family relationships that stretched over hundreds of kilometres in East Arnhem Land and an advanced intellectual language that early anthropologists did not know. An energy filled Cassie as Mike headed down toward the art centre. The ancient land of mysterious songs, dances and didgeridoo rhythms had already engulfed Cassie. Her spirit soared even higher as she saw an eagle circling over a building site, where Yolngu men were digging trenches and carrying pieces of timber.

"Come and I'll introduce you to Ben, he's training up a local building team."

Cassie forced a polite smile as she took Ben's rough hand in a firm grip.

"Yes, we've already met," said Ben as he returned her weak smile with his own, his intense brown eyes not leaving Cassie's.

"Ben's going to see what he can do to fix up bits of the art centre for you ..."

"Only in between building these houses Mike. You know I was only hired to train up the Yolngu building team."

"That's right, that's right Ben, but we've talked about this – some of the men could do that white ant repair and sort out the plumbing."

Cassie stayed quiet as she watched the two men have some kind of power play. She couldn't help but contrast Mike's middle-aged soft belly and arms with Ben's broad shoulders and tanned strong forearms, maybe even more brown than her own.

Ben looked at her again with those piercing eyes and Cassie noticed that his two thumbs were locked firmly in the belt of his shorts as he spoke.

"I'll come round sometime mid-morning tomorrow and we'll have a look see what needs to be done. Is that okay with you Cassie?"

Cassie was somewhat taken aback by this new polite Ben, yet he was distracting her by not breaking his gaze into her eyes.

"That should be fine Ben. I hope to have some sort of rough operational plan for the art centre by then." Cassie paused and blushed slightly as she looked down at the ground and Ben's legs. "I just want you to know that I'm really sorry about yesterday. Look, I'm also really good with fibreglass. My dad taught me how to lay glass and I've made quite a few fibreglass sculptures back home," she added hopefully.

Ben paused before answering. Today in the bright sunlight, he saw a woman with a beautiful face and outfit that emphasised her gentle curves. *They were in all the right places*, he thought and he couldn't hold back the smile that was usually on his face.

"I can't pretend to say it's alright. Maybe we can sort something out this weekend?" His eyebrows rose as he rubbed his slightly crooked nose.

"Okay, it's a deal. That will give me a chance to settle into my new house. Is it anywhere nearby Mike?"

"It's right behind the art centre. I'll let Karen show you round later, she's your assistant."

Ben had already returned to work as they drove off down the hill toward the art centre. Cassie shot a quick glance in Ben's direction, only to notice the full definition in Ben's leg muscles and arms as he crouched to pick up some forming boards. She sighed to herself, but resolved not to let herself be distracted. After all, she had a job to do.

"Cassie Greenway, this is Karen Kumani. Karen can fill you in on the history of the art centre and show you how we do things around here." Mike grinned as he placed a soft hand in the small of each woman's back while they were shaking hands. That was not the first time Cassie noted he had invaded her unspecified personal space. She stepped away slightly, returning Karen's warm smile while noticing Karen's sideways glance and slight grimace in Mike's direction.

"Well, I'll have to love you and leave you ladies," chortled Mike, his belly shaking at his own joke, "Lots to do today, council meeting next week – I'll talk to you about that soon Cassie." With that, he turned and walked back to his car, lurching from side to side with each step.

"Let me show you around Cassie. This is your office, you might like to put your things in there?" said Karen indicating a diminutive room with an ancient wooden table, a new looking swivel office chair and a filing cabinet. A dust covered computer sat on a side desk strewn with pieces of paper. She made a mental note of all the cleaning and re-arranging she would do to organise things properly. Living on a boat for several months had made her even more particular about putting things away in the correct place.

As Karen led her into the galleries, Cassie observed Karen's willowy walk and bare feet just as she had seen earlier with the lithesome Yolngu women. She either had a perfect tan or was part aboriginal with European features. Her long black hair swayed over her shoulders as she gave a running commentary of the art works.

"And these bark paintings are by George Dumatja. You'll meet him soon; he's coming in this afternoon to see you. 'E's one of the twelve clan leaders – 'e's a bossy bloke, but 'is paintings sell for over $5,000 each. There's some Japanese clients that really go for his stuff. Thing is, 'e gets on the gunja a bit, then you don't want to know." Karen seemed suddenly agitated as she spoke.

"What do you mean he gets on the gunja? Karen?"

"Sorry, he smokes a bit of marijuana. Bashes up 'is poor wife too when 'e's like that. No worries though, I reckon I can handle him now," a nervous grin exposed her perfect teeth between sensual full lips. "Cup of tea?"

"Yes please. White no sugar" said Cassie as she followed Karen into a side room.

"This is my cubby hole. It's also the store room and where we pack off art works to mail off to people."

Cassie began to feel more relaxed as she sipped the hot tea and nibbled a Scottish shortbread.

"Tell me about yourself Karen. How long have you been here and where are you from?"

"Yeah, I've been 'ere about a year. I came up with me boyfriend from Alice Springs, but he shot through a few months ago. Good riddance too, good for nothing creep. He was doin' Ben's job for a while, but the Yolngu didn't like him much. Sat on his arse barkin' orders most of the time. Hey that Ben's a good sort. Have ya seen him yet?"

Cassie smiled and became aware of the paradox in Karen's fine pretty features and unrefined speech.

"Yes, I've met him. Actually, I smashed my boat into his when I arrived. He's still pretty mad at me." Cassie winced slightly as she recalled their disastrous meeting.

"Yeah, I heard about that from Mario" said Karen enthusiastically. "Ben's a good bloke though – thing is, I don't think he likes women, you know, too much."

"What do you mean; you're not saying he's gay are you?"

"No, no, I don't think so. I mean I've been trying to catch him ever since Gary left. Gary was me last boyfriend. But he just won't be caught! I mean, he's funny and good to talk to – e's just different really. I've never met anyone like him before."

With such openness, Cassie felt she could let her guard down with Karen. She liked her straightforward and honest outlook.

"Well, I don't think he's very nice Karen" said Cassie quietly. "You should have heard the vile things he said to me when I was lying on my deck, bleeding from the nose. This is after I'd spent three months sailing across the Pacific to get here!"

"Wow, that doesn't sound like the Ben I've seen" said Karen. "Do you know he spends a lot of time at Garrawarra's place, out at North Bay Beach?"

"Who's Garra, Garrawarra?" asked Cassie uncertainly.

"Henry Garrawarra. He's foreman of Ben's building team. E's being groomed for clan leadership, smart young guy, really gets his blokes workin'. Now if *he* wasn't married with kids!"

"I've heard it takes a while for Yolngu to trust you and take you into their homes?" Cassie raised her eyebrows inquisitively.

"Yeah, but Ben's different. He got adopted straight away. I know he takes presents for kids like clothes and toys and he often sits on the cliff top there with the old men and Garrawarra, just talkin' or watching ceremony practice. I've never known other white fellas to do that."

Cassie sat quietly for a moment, pondering what she had heard. Could she be wrong about Ben? She quickly dismissed these thoughts.

"I don't know Karen; I think actions speak louder than words. But tell me, what do you know about Mario? He seems nice?"

"Yeah, don't think he likes dark girls like me. E's always chasin' after every new white nurse that comes to work in the clinic though."

"Really? Guess I'm not surprised. I know he's been married before, apparently a rich lady from Sydney."

"Yeah, a real cow I heard – but Ben's been married before too. Don't know any more though. He won't talk about it."

"Sounds like you really fancy Ben, Karen?"

"Wouldn't mind a piece of that – have you seen his legs?"

Cassie crossed hers uncomfortably, eager to change the subject,

"So you haven't said yet where you're from?"

Karen spent a while talking about her Scottish father, a teacher who had met an aboriginal nurse in Alice Springs. They had married and Karen and her brothers were the result. She had been interested in art from childhood and had studied fine arts in Darwin, but never finished and had only done odd jobs around Darwin, before she came to Umbakala with Gary.

Suddenly Karen stood up as a middle aged Yolngu woman came into the room.

"Namirri Yapa, this is our new boss, Cassie" said Karen introducing Cassie to the short round woman with a mass of black curly hair sprinkled with white strands.

"Cassie, this is Rose Wamatta. She's one of the artists and also your housekeeper."

They exchanged smiles and shook hands. Rose looked down shyly as Cassie noted the bright bougainvillea flowers painted on her broad yellow dress.

"Did you design that dress pattern Rose?" A long pause.

"Yes ... I paint on material. Do bark painting too."
Karen interrupted quickly, now appearing slightly impatient.

"If it's okay with you Cassie, Rose can help you bring your stuff up to your house now. I've got a few orders to send off?"

"Sounds great Karen. Just a couple of bags for now. Shall we go Rose?"

"Yo, we go yapa."

"Tell me Rose, what does yo and yapa mean?"

"Yo mean yes and yapa mean woman."

"Perhaps you can teach me some more language while we're walking?" added Cassie. With more smiles all round, they headed off to the boat.

It was stifling outside the art centre. Cassie could see heat waves glistening on the red gravel road. A short while later, they had slowly climbed the outside stairs onto a shaded verandah. Bright purple Bougainvillea engulfed the stair railing and looking beyond the profusion, Cassie marvelled at the intense blue of the Arafura Sea beyond the bay, rising up to meet an equally blue sky. The perfume of the white frangipani flowers from the tree beside the house overwhelmed her for a brief moment as she closed her eyes and breathed in the power of the scent.

Inside was an open living room and kitchen with an elegantly polished timber floor. Two large fans turned lazily in the ceiling and two bedrooms opened up to the rear of the house. This was far better than Cassie had expected.

While they unpacked Cassie's bags, Rose proudly told her how her husband, Peter Bulangi was a cultural elder and also a councillor. She also talked about how George Dumatja was the art centre cultural leader, but said nothing about his nature that Karen had revealed.

"I make you some lunch Cassie. Mike say to get bread and few things for you. Council pay," said Rose in a monotone.

"Thank you Rose, I'll just unpack while you do that. You'll join me for lunch won't you?"

"Yo ..." she trailed off, walking into the familiar kitchen.

Cassie had nearly finished sorting her things when she heard soft but powerful footsteps, followed by the screen door slamming. She heard Yolngu words and a man's voice as she stepped into the living room to see a tall, wiry black man with greying curly hair. He wore a black t-shirt and dirty paint stained jeans, which were too short for his long legs. As Cassie appeared he stopped shouting at Rose, who with head lowered was spreading butter on sandwiches. His piercing black eyes were wide as he stared at Cassie. Flaring nostrils reminded Cassie of the wild bulls she had seen years ago in Spain.

"Who you lady? You new art centre manager?" he shouted, fists clenched by his side, still staring into Cassie's eyes. Cassie trembled, mustering every ounce of composure she could. She tried not to show her fear through her eyes. Her hands behind her back started shaking as the man slowly walked toward her.

"You got my money lady?"

"I ... I don't know what money you mean ... I only got ...."

"My money for painting ... where is it? You give me now!"

"I'm sorry; I'll talk to Karen and find out for you. Who are you anyway?"

Cassie soon realised it must have been the wrong question, because in one swift move, with eyes even wider, he leapt forward, cupped his long fingered hand around her throat and pushed her back against the wall in an iron grip. His breath was like rancid meat as he spoke through clenched teeth.

"I want money ... two days lady. I clan leader, need money for funeral ... brother die in Ramingining ..." Cassie's eyes were round and open, arms powerless by her side, her breathing shallow.

Just as quickly as he had grabbed her, Dumatja released her and sprang across the room like a dingo. He turned and raised the corners of his mouth. *Was it a grin?* thought Cassie.

"Two days lady ... I come back."

Rose rushed over to Cassie, who was doubled over, rubbing her neck. There were red welts on either side and her veins were now pulsing with relief.

"I take it that was George Dumatja?" Cassie asked smiling. She laughed privately because of that involuntary smile and thought about people laughing or smiling in moments of fear or terror.

"Yo, he bad man miss. He very powerful man ... better do as he say miss."

Cassie walked slowly over to the kitchen while Rose poured out two cups of tea. She watched silently as Rose heaped three large teaspoons of sugar into each cup. She wondered what she had gotten herself into. This was so different to her comfortable life teaching high school art in San Francisco.

3 Sir Galahad

The tuna sandwich Ben munched seemed chewy and tasteless. He sat alone on the building site while his workers had either gone home or to a takeaway to have their own lunch. Lunch time was a chance for Ben to gather his thoughts and plan his building activities in his head but today he was disgruntled. He struggled with the idea of repairing the art centre. *That woman's going to be more trouble. First she wrecks my boat, now she's going to demand I fix up her building – I just know it.* As he put away his plastic lunch box, Ben looked up to see a battered white Troopy come tearing round the corner from the direction of Cassie's place. He gazed at the speeding car and for a brief moment, his eyes locked with George Dumatja's angry face. *What's he up to, driving like a loony?* thought Ben. Dumatja, like all the locals, usually drove slowly through town.

It was still half an hour before nightfall and Ben waited impatiently for his pressure cooker, steaming the smell of curried rice and fish into his galley. He kept looking at the gaping hole in the hull as he gobbled his dinner, hardly chewing a single bite. His small plastic mug of merlot disguised some of the taste of his less than perfect cooking. Although it was a dry community, with alcohol banned for the Yolngu, outsiders and white workers were allowed to drink in their own homes. Ben knew from talking to the old men, the clan leaders, how alcohol had led to family violence and child abuse. He shared their concerns about the sale of the kava drug by the council and marijuana by an enterprising senior man in Umbakala. Tonight again, he was going to meet with some of the good men, including his foreman, Garrawarra. This group met quite often, all keen to make a difference in their community.

The sun was an orange blanket over the Arafura Sea when Ben walked swiftly up the path toward town. As he walked past the art centre, he made a mental note about his meeting with Cassie, when they would talk about repairing the damaged beams and plumbing. He became irritated as he remembered the argument with Mike. Mike did not understand that he needed to be almost constantly with his crew to train them and supervise their work. Two locations would make it very difficult. He did not how it would be possible to do both jobs but despite himself, was reluctant to say no. Umbakala really needed the art centre to be a success for their community to flourish.

Ben looked up as he passed the art centre house. Cassie was there in the kitchen window a halo of light surrounding her brown hair. He quickly looked away pretending he hadn't seen her as his heart thumped in his chest. He rationalised that he was just walking fast up the steep path. *She was not going to get under his skin, no way.*

"Hello Ben." He was startled by a dusky woman's voice from behind in the shadows. Ben swung around and saw Karen.

"Hi Karen, where are you off to?"

"I was just goin' for a walk, needed to get out after wrappin' art orders all arvo." Karen hoped her reason sounded credible. She knew that Ben quite often went to the North Bay camp to sit with the elders after dusk.

"I'm just off to see Garrawarra and some of the old men – sorry, can't really stay and chat" said Ben in his usual friendly manner. He couldn't help but notice how beautiful Karen looked in her low-cut floaty dress. He was always a bit nervous around beautiful women, until he came to know them better, and Karen was no exception.

"I'll walk up there with you if you don't mind? That is, if you can keep up with me!" Karen dashed off ahead laughing, hair swirling seductively as she looked back at Ben.

"Keep up?" said Ben as he accelerated in his steel capped work boots, "Sprint champion at Toongabbie primary school I'll have you know!"

As he passed Karen easily, he felt her arms grab around his waist in a mock football tackle. He swung round and his eyes connected with Cassie's in the window again, before they came to a stop on Karen's cheeky expression. In the fading light he saw Mario stepping through the front gate of Cassie's house.

"Yeah, I'll bet you were captain of the girl's netball team too, eh Ben?" Karen teased.

"Well at least the girls at our school didn't play rugby," he said, still conscious of Cassie's searching eyes at the window. "Where did you learn to tackle like that?" asked Ben, his breath steadying, as they continued walking along the path toward the town.

"I've had three younger brothers, I mean; I still have three younger brothers. We were always out in the backyard playing footy or cricket. Dad would join in when he came home from work. I can kick a ball pretty good too – we ought to have a go on the beach one day eh?"

Ben smiled as he looked across at this slender woman and tried to imagine her kicking a football in her long dress.

"I'll give you a fiver if you can kick a footy more than ten yards in that dress!" he replied laughing.

"Hey you're right. Well then, I'll just have to take it off then – but you won't be allowed to look." She grinned back at Ben, pleased as the flirting reached a new level.

Ben hoped Karen would not notice the blood rushing to his cheeks as he pictured Karen kicking a football. He smiled back, the words not coming to continue this line of revelry. He held back, he decided he mustn't lead her on. *Not now, not now, I just can't do this.*

"What about you Ben? Were you really any good at sprinting?"

Ben looked at the ground as they walked, pausing before he answered – he replied, a humble tone in his voice. "Well, I was always a sportaholic, tried just about every sport. You were half right though, it wasn't netball, it was basketball I was good at, although I did play a bit of rugby at school as well."

"Yeah, I thought so, you had to get those sexy legs somehow!" exclaimed Karen boldly stepping up the ante as she stopped, hands on her hips, legs spread and a big grin on her face. Before Ben could reply and perhaps sensing she had gone too far, Karen said, "Listen – I gotta go and make some dinner. See ya tomorrow? Cassie said you'd be comin' round to look at the art centre? That right?"

"Sure will," said Ben with a half-smile.

"Okay – byee," Karen almost sang as she spun around with a wave of her hand and disappeared into the gloom. Ben felt flattered and somewhat elated by her attentions, but there was no way he wanted any sort of complications with Karen, as beautiful as she was. Still, that little diversion on the track was only a bit of fun. *Just a bit of fun, that's all,* he pondered. He just hoped she saw it like that.

Ben resumed his walk along the bush, past the lights and sounds from the houses on his right, the quiet of the bay on his left. Soon he saw the flickering of a fire where he knew his friends would be sitting. On the clifftop were about 20 women, their brightly patterned dresses faded in the dim light glowing on Garrawarra's verandah. *Ceremony practice*, he thought, *must be another funeral.*

"Namirri Ben," came the nasally welcome from Charlie Alanja. He was sitting beside the fire, cross-legged and bare-chested. His white teeth and fiery coal eyes were encircled by the white ochre paint on his cheeks and forehead.

"Namirri Alanja." Ben returned the smile, noticing for the first time Alanja's manhood initiation scars, like small black snakes glued to his chest. As he sat next to Alanja, he noticed Garrawarra and Peter Bulangi talking earnestly near the gathering of women. A third man Ben had never seen before sat on a chair nearby. He was Yolngu, but dressed in long grey trousers, black leather shoes and a colourful floral shirt.

"What's with the spears uncle?" Ben asked, while nodding towards a small pile of spears – fresh white wood and thin strips of bark on the ground.

"Making them for funeral. Rose Wamatta's mother die – my aunty. She 74 – pretty good for Yolngu eh?"

Ben nodded his head, acknowledging the irony in this statement. He knew that poor western diets of white flour, sugar and fatty foods from the takeaways meant that they were lucky to live past fifty. Garrawarra and Bulangi were suddenly beside them, looking solemn.

"Sorry to hear about your mother in law Bulangi," Ben didn't know what else to say. He knew he had only started to learn about the complex Yolngu cultural ways.

"Thank you Ben. We already planning funeral, starting ceremony practice with women. Some young women still learning. You stay if you like – you welcome Ben. We don't get white fella come and sit in sand and talk with us."

"I enjoy your company fellas – you've already taught me so much I didn't know."

"We reckon maybe you can help us Ben, not like that last bloke," smiled Garrawarra. "Don't just mean showin' us 'ow to build houses. I know I was just a boy when government give us sit down money and all started to go bad."

Ben knew he was talking about the early seventies, when the Australian government kicked out the missionaries and gave the remote aboriginal people the dole.

"That's right," said Alanja. "Bulangi here was a mechanic, could fix anything. I was fisherman. Our clan caught lot of fish in this big wooden boat. Not now. All young fellas do now – drink kava, smoke gunja and play cards all day."

The others nodded sagely while staring into the fire.

"You blokes are on the council," said Ben. "Why don't you stop bringing in building contractors from Darwin? Your own people are putting down your workers when they see how quickly the outside contractors build homes. We just need time to get your blokes up to speed and off the gunja."

"We jus' don't understand white fella government way Ben. Mike say we have no choice. Have to have twelve month government contract."

Again, Ben felt weighed down by the frustration of his work here. He was someone who would identify a problem and just solve it. These series of paradoxes were not easy to deal with. In the background a set of clap sticks started a typical Yolngu beat. The shadows hid a man who was singing as the women began to dance, swaying their hips and moving their feet in the dust, like slender footed deer performing a moonwalking dance. The effect was unique. Ben sat in awe watching, mesmerised by their graceful movements, while the well-dressed black man at the front seemed to be teaching the women the subtlety of the movements.

"That turtle dance Ben," said Alanja, as if that explained everything.

"Anyway Ben, we need to get men working again," said Bulangi, changing the subject back.

"What about your traditional laws?" asked Ben.

"You mean spear 'im in leg if 'e don't work?" laughed Garrawarra. Ben noticed that the old men weren't smiling. Alanja looked across to Garrawarra, his eyes narrowing, the warrior paint making him look fierce in the flickering fire light.

"We bring back law if white fella police don't stop bad fellas. In old days, we spear that man selling gunja and taking women not his. Not in leg – we kill him. One clan leader. One strong man."

The group went quiet with Alanja's exclamation. Ben shivered a little at the idea of capital punishment by spearing.

It was after eleven when Ben bid his farewells and made his way back along the well-worn path skirting the village. As he passed Cassie's house, he saw that the lights were out. All was dark at the Boatyard too where normally Mario would be sitting in front of a flickering TV. Ben thought about Mario. *Was he spending the night?* He dismissed a sudden irrational pang of jealousy. After all, it was none of his business and Cassie may be pretty but she seemed like a whole heap of trouble.

Cassie gingerly replaced the handset, as if it was a piece of fine china. After George Dumatja's visit, she had returned to the art centre and phoned Mike straight away. She had expected Mike to be outraged and call the police immediately, but somehow Mike had played down the incident, saying that he would take care of it and talk to Dumatja. Cassie could feel her lip tremble but she fought back the tears while talking to Mike. Her mother had confessed her concern to Cassie last year that she never cried, even when she was a little girl. That time she had slid down the rope out of the treehouse and burnt her hands, or the day she cut her foot on jagged glass – she hadn't cried. Her mother expected to console Cassie when she broke off with James, but again, there were no tears. Now, she was just too angry to cry. *How dare Mike try to brush this off as if it were nothing?*

After the call, Karen came into Cassie's office. She had been busy packing orders and hadn't noticed Cassie's arrival at the art centre until she heard the anger in Cassie's voice as she was telling Mike about Dumatja's attack.

"Are you alright Cassie? I heard you talkin' to Mike, are you okay? What's he gonna do about it?" Karen looked anxiously at the welts on Cassie's neck.

"I'm not sure Karen; I'm not really hurt, just frightened of what else he might do. He said he wanted money, do we owe him money?"

"He's always after money. The last manager? 'E was a bit soft and paid him for paintings before they were sold. Everyone else only got their money after their stuff sold," said Karen quietly.

"What about the police?" asked Cassie, eyebrows raised.

"Huh, police? There's a station way off at Nhulunbuy, but we've only got local patrols. They can't touch the elders. Dumatja is a strong man. In the old days, the other clan leaders would have dealt with him, but now – 'e just does what 'e wants."

"Has he ever done anything to you Karen?"
Karen's eyes glazed over as she seemed to look right through Cassie. There was a long pause before she answered.

"Nah, I just tell him I'm not allowed to give out money and just tell him to go and see Mike."
For the first time Cassie wasn't convinced Karen was telling the truth. There was something Karen wasn't telling her.

"Well, I suppose there's nothing to worry about as long as Mike can sort it out. I just hope he does it quickly. Anyway, better get some work done. Look, I want to spend the rest of the afternoon checking out our stock and our artist's profiles. Can you help me with that Karen?"

"No worries boss!" she replied with, what appeared to Cassie, false bravado.

Cassie spent the afternoon studying the operation, making notes and planning an artist's meeting so she could get to know them personally. Her dad had taught her about relationship building with the antique business. Even as a teenager, Cassie enjoyed meeting people. When she was seventeen, her dad had sent her to value and make an offer on the antique furniture that filled one lady's house. To Cassie it had been the most natural thing to sit and listen to the old lady's stories, her life, her furniture pieces. She didn't really care about the profits; Cassie just wanted to give the lady a fair price for her prized possessions. Her father was delighted when Cassie had told her about the deal and that the old lady had agreed to write some history about each piece. Here in Arnhem Land, Cassie was going to do the same thing. She would find out more of the history of each artist and print off pages of their thoughts and ideas and backgrounds. She was sure it would be a good way to promote their work. Her father's words of wisdom about business came back to her vividly. 'Look after the people and the money will come.'

"Namirri Cassie." It was Rose who startled Cassie as she was closing up the last artist file. Cassie had already scrutinised Dumatja's file. There was little written about him, but his art was powerful.

"Sorry miss. I came to see if you alright?"

"Thanks Rose, yep – Mike said he'd sort out Dumatja. Do you think I'll be safe in my own house tonight?"

"Not sure Miss Cassie. He very bad man. Not sure."

The sun was low as Rose walked Cassie back to her house. Karen had left earlier saying she had to meet someone.

"Thanks for walking with me Rose. I'll be alright. See you tomorrow, okay?"

Rose gave a warm but sad smile before she walked off in the direction of her home. Cassie quickly locked the door behind her. The windows were open and fitted with insect screens. She checked the locks. Cassie turned on the ceiling fans and decided it was too hot to shut the windows, but still worried that she was here alone. She felt vulnerable and weak as she opened the kitchen drawers and found three sharp knives, grabbing a deadly looking carving knife. Not that she could have used it, but she hoped it might frighten off Dumatja if he returned when she was alone. Her knuckles were white and she gritted her teeth as she looked across at the wall where she had been held captive earlier that day. She saw the telephone, one of those old fashioned plastic boxes where you spun the dial to ring out. There was a small photocopied booklet next to the phone, 'Umbakala' phone listings'. Urgently, she flicked through it, looking under 'B', 'boatyard', there it was. Mario Bestoni. Cassie rang the number, not quite sure what she was going to say. The phone kept ringing and ringing. Cassie was about to hang up when finally, she heard Mario's voice.

"G'day, Mario here."

"H-hi Mario. It's Cassie. Can you talk?"

"Hey gorgeous! I was just gettin' in the shower. Can I talk – me? You know me, talk the legs off a table, I would. What's up, couldn't live another minute without me eh?"

"Something happened today Mario. I'm a bit frightened. Can you come over? Look, how about I make you some dinner – Rose stocked me up with groceries. I should be able to whip something up."

"Just give me ten minutes. Hey, I just got out some pasta and beer; can I bring that over?"

"Sure Mario, see you soon."

Mario showered off the day's grime. He had been sanding fibreglass all day and was covered in fine white dust. He decided to reach for a small bottle of aftershave, spraying under his arms, then as an afterthought, wafted some down the front of his shorts for good luck. The last time he did that was two months ago. Joanne was a very willing nurse who came to dinner and stayed. Mario remembered they had beer and pasta that night as well. *Hmm, things are looking promising.*

As Mario opened the gate into Cassie's yard, he glimpsed Ben and Karen in the distance. It looked like they were dancing and he could hear their breathless giggles. He nearly called out to them, but decided against advertising that he was here. *After all, four is a crowd*, he thought, as he bounded up the verandah stairs, two at a time.

"Hello gorgeous," said Mario with a broad grin on his face as he handed Cassie a packaged pasta meal for two and a large bottle of beer. It was still cold and misted in the heat of the evening. Cassie smiled back, but said nothing as she locked the door behind Mario.

"Hey, you don't have to lock doors in Umbakala, no one's going to steal from you, you know. The Yolngu will take stuff from each other, but that's just their culture of sharing."

Cassie paused, the frown line between her eyes deepened, her arms crossed tightly under her breasts.

"That's not what worries me Mario. I-I was attacked earlier today and don't want it to happen again." She blinked away the tears as he took her in his arms.

After Cassie had explained what had happened, they sat quietly on the couch, staring straight ahead into nothingness.

"Gee Cassie, I knew he was a bit of a bad dude, bashing up his wife and fooling around with some of the single women, but never heard of a Yolngu having a go at a white woman – or man really. This is a whole new ball game."

Cassie started to warm up the food, tipping the contents of the once frozen pasta into a saucepan and lighting the gas stove. She chopped up some frozen broccoli, the nearest thing to fresh vegetables she could find in the local shops, and out of the corner of her eye watched Mario sitting quietly on the couch, head in his hands. He had changed, his bravado was gone.

"So what do you think Mario? You grew up with these people – am I in danger here?"

Mario looked at Cassie, unsmiling, his brow creased.

"I don't know where to begin Cassie," he said flatly, no enthusiasm in his voice now. "Look, it's not the physical stuff I'm worried about, it's the other stuff."

"What do you mean; other stuff?" quizzed Cassie as she slowly stirred the pot.

Mario paused for what seemed an endless time before answering.

"When I was about eighteen, one of my friends died. He was Yolngu. He started, let's say, spending time with a girl, it was actually Dumatja's daughter. It should have been okay though – he was Duhwa, she was Yirritja." Mario then described in great detail how when a Yolngu baby was born, it was slotted into a complex chart, a logical maze where everyone had their place. This chart was known by all Yolngu in their heads. They were either one of two moieties, Dhuwa or Yirritja; they could only marry outside their own moiety. A Dhuwa person could only marry a Yirritja person, but from birth, each child was destined to marry only one other from that chart. Mario explained how angry Dumatja was and he had warned his friend to leave his daughter alone.

"So what has this to do with my attack Mario?" said Cassie impatiently. She was intrigued to know more about this part of the Yolngu culture but right now, she just wanted to feel safe.

"I'm coming to that," said Mario. "Anyway, when Dumatja found out they were still seeing each other; he put a curse on my friend."

"Are you telling me your friend died from a curse?" asked Cassie, her mouth wide open as her eye's questioned Mario.

"Yeah. He j-just got sick. The doctor didn't know what was wrong with him. They even sent him by flying doctor to Darwin in the end. He died there in hospital."

"You think he's like, like a witch doctor then?" asked Cassie.

"Something like that, but near as I can make out, the higher they get in the 'knowledge' stuff, the more they get into spiritual stuff I don't understand. They say they can talk to their ancestors and that the spirits can do stuff for them."

"Like kill amorous young men?"

"Exactly."

They sat quietly for most of the meal. The mood from the first night when they ate at Mario's boat house had changed. Mario seemed different now. No longer the brash would-be seducer. It was like he was entranced by the spirit warriors of Umbakala himself. It was then they heard the clap sticks, the hollow sound of the smooth polished instruments, like fossilised French bread sticks, accompanied by the wailing mournful song. Cassie shivered despite the heat of the night.

"They're mourning Rose Wamatta's mother" said Mario quietly.

"Rose's mother? She didn't tell me her mother had died," said Cassie with a surprised lilt in her voice.

"No – she wouldn't. But there's something you should know. Her dead mother's name was, Gundwarri, Betty Gundwarri, but you must *never* say her name in the presence of Yolngu. It's taboo."

Cassie didn't ask why, she just sipped on her cold beer allowing the bubbles to drift quietly into her brain, calming, soothing her spirit. She started to feel safe with Mario here. Earlier she had been worried he might make advances, but not any more. He agreed to stay the night in the spare room with the door open so that he would hopefully hear anyone coming first. After a quick shower, Cassie locked her own bedroom door behind her and checked the windows again. She noted that it was only a modern lightweight door, no match for a Yolngu witch doctor's shoulder, but at least Mario was near.

Cassie tossed from side to side on the light cotton sheets. She couldn't bring herself to sleep naked in the heat like she had on the boat and wore a pair of short frilly pyjamas her mother had given her as a parting gift. She had wondered when on earth she'd wear them but now somehow she felt reassured to have this reminder of home. The fan was humming and through the open window she heard the faint sound of rock music. The traditional songs had stopped and this had taken its place. She recognised the music from the Doors, 'Don't you love her madly ...' Cassie smiled just before she fell asleep. It was one of her favourite songs.

The sun splashed a single beam of hope onto Cassie's face the next morning. Her legs were tangled in the sheet and she was curled in the foetal position. It was cooler now and she almost felt like pulling up the light blanket that had slipped to the floor. Cassie heard familiar clattering noises in the kitchen. *That would be Mario*, she decided, *he must be making breakfast*. Cassie flung her legs skyward, levering herself out of bed and over to her wardrobe. She had brought with her a selection of long summer skirts and blouses and quickly chose an outfit before brushing the tousles out of her naturally wavy brown hair. She looked at the make-up bag and decided not to bother. *Too hot for make-up*, but she grabbed some roll-on deodorant and applied it under her loose white blouse. Satisfied with her preparations, Cassie tried to quietly unlock the door, not wanting Mario to think she didn't trust him.

"Morning gorgeous!" Mario was in high spirits again, "I was going to knock on your door. I've made some pancakes and coffee. Is that okay? There's marmalade and strawberry jam here to go with it."

"Thanks Mario, that's so sweet. I don't know how I can thank you."

"I'll think of something" said Mario with a wink and a wicked grin on his face. He then quickly reached out and grabbed her round the waist, his face coming closer to hers. Their lips were about to collide, when Cassie overcame the shock and turned her head to one side. She squeezed two hands onto his chest and gently eased him away, but collected a peck on her cheek. It felt good to be touched and held by strong arms and Cassie struggled not to submit as she smelled his skin and a scent she recognised.

"Steady on fella – just friends okay?" as she stepped aside and grabbed the coffee plunger.

"Friends? Sure Cassie, whatever you say. Come on grab a seat while they're still hot – the pancakes I mean." Mario laughed at his own joke. Cassie didn't know if it was nervous laughter or if his lunge had meant nothing to him. *Was she just another pretty girl to kiss?* In a way he reminded her of the college jocks who dated all the girls and seemed to want nothing but sex. Not that Mario was unappealing, he certainly had sex appeal. *Not now, not now,* said Cassie to herself, flattered, but not ready to get involved with a man. Not yet anyway.

Mario had earned another tick in her man box after that delicious breakfast. He had put sultanas in the batter and fried them to a golden brown colour until they were light and fluffy. *Even my dad couldn't have done better,* thought Cassie as she skipped down the stairs and into her small garden.

"Hey, wait for me," cried Mario with a muffled voice, still chomping on the last pancake. "I'll walk you to the door of the art centre."

"Sir Galahad," laughed Cassie, "or is it Don Quixote?"

"Don who?" mumbled Mario, still chewing.

"Never mind." She could see there were gaps in Mario's education, but Cassie reassured herself that least he must have known who Galahad was.

Mario walked off to the boatyard after he saw Cassie into the art centre. She watched him as he disappeared, screened by the distance and the light gum trees. He had an unusual walk, didn't swing his arms much, Cassie noted before she was disturbed by someone singing. It was a man's voice and the sound was coming from the road further away from the cliff top. "Don't you love her madly, don't you need her badly, don't you love her ways .....". It was Ben heading off to the building site. Cassie quickly ducked down behind a squat Grevillia bush; she didn't want Ben to know she was watching him. *He must have heard the song last night as well,* she thought. *Funny how a tune can get into your head and not want to leave.*

Cassie was still humming the same tune two hours later when Karen arrived at work. It was nine fifteen again, noted Cassie. It was time to talk to Karen about work hours. Mario had told her about 'Yolngu time'. Punctuality, appointed times didn't really exist here. It sounded a bit like the Spanish 'Manyana'. Things would happen, but in their own time. Cassie sensed Karen was a good worker and knew that she would have to be diplomatic and maybe accept how things were done here. Maybe even just accept 'Yolngu time'?

"Morning Boss," chirped Karen, "How are you this morning, did you sleep okay?"

"Good morning Karen. Yes thanks," she lied, "I've been here for ages checking on the stock records and sales. Have you got a minute so we can go over them together?"

"Sure thing Cassie, I'll just grab a coffee and some toast – would you like some?"

For the next hour they chatted about the job. Karen had agreed reluctantly to try to keep normal hours adding that her last boss didn't care when she came in and that Mike was the same. People in the council office came in when they were ready.

"I don't know about the last stock take Cassie, I'm not real good with numbers."

"The figures just don't add up Karen – I don't understand. These computer statements from the office just don't add up to your hand-written sales ledger."

Karen looked a bit guilty and raised her voice slightly. *Mild indignation*, thought Cassie.

"I don't know anything about that. I just take up the bag of cash and credit card slips each day to the office. They take up the internet sales. It's usually Mike that gets them – or the book-keeper. I do me best Cassie – honest!"

Cassie looked at the neatly written numbers in the sales ledger. They were childlike yet meticulous. There was a naivety in each zero, an almost perfect circle, sitting neatly and exactly on the line. Cassie smiled and put her hand gently on Karen's arm.

"No one's accusing you of anything Karen; it's just that the figures don't balance. The reports from the office show less sales than our ledger, that's all. I'll check with Mike about it – better still, I'll meet up with the book-keeper. I'm sure we'll be able to sort it out."

"Thanks Cassie," she said quietly. "I do me best."

"I know you do Karen. Only Mike says the art centre's in financial difficulty, so we need to do what we can to make sure it's profitable. I think we can."

"No worries Cassie. If it's okay with you, I'll put some more stock out. There's a tourist group coming in by bus this arvo from Nhulunbuy. Oh and don't forget Ben's comin' this mornin' to look at the building," she said excitedly, grinning, as she skipped off to the store room where the acrylics on paper and ochre on bark paintings were stored on deep shelves. *Oh, so that's why she's got on her lippy today*, Cassie mused.

Cassie had forgotten about Ben's visit. The plumbing certainly needed fixing and there were two whole walls out of action where the lining had been ripped off so the termites could be poisoned. She found some more shortbread biscuits in the cupboard and real coffee next to a plunger Karen had left out. She would make an extra effort to be hospitable to Ben in spite of his bad manners. Then she suddenly remembered how playful Ben had been last night on the path near her place with Karen. *Looks like Karen might be getting what she wants after all?* She secretly hoped Ben would be in a good mood this morning – she didn't need any more enemies – Dumatja was enough.

4   The Poem

By mid-morning, Cassie had taken a break from her management research and was working with Karen to rearrange the displays. It was the first time she had a chance to examine closely the fine weave of the baskets and mats, the exquisite carvings and ornate didgeridoos. She noticed that most of the painting was now done with acrylic paints on paper instead of clay paint on bark. *Sign of the times,* she thought, but at least they were more convenient to pack and mail off to customers all over the world. She made her first sale that morning to a Norwegian couple who had flown in by charter plane from Darwin. No shortage of money there and they bought a number of works, even one of Dumatja's more expensive ones. Cassie felt some relief at the sale of his work, hoping that would enable Dumatja to get all the money he might need for a while. Relieved also that they paid by credit card, so the money would go straight into the bank account.

Just after they left, there was a knock at the front door, followed by heavy footsteps. Cassie spun around to see Ben's large frame standing there, hat in hand, almost like a schoolboy who had been sent to the headmaster. The body language puzzled Cassie as she stepped toward him, feeling a sudden tightening in her chest. Her mouth was dry as she spoke politely.

"Thanks for coming Ben. I know how busy you must be."

"That's okay Cassie, the boys are having a smoko anyway ..." He hadn't finished his sentence when Karen padded up to Ben with a flourish of skirts and hair.

"Hi Ben, I see you got away from the corroborree then?"
Ben smiled warmly, now ignoring Cassie,

"Nothing to get away from Karen, those old men are my friends – but look, I can't hang around, I've got to have a look at the job here."
Cassie interrupted, mild annoyance in her voice,

"Karen, do you mind getting on with that jewellery display please? Ben and I need to talk."

"Sure thing – see ya later Ben," said Karen as she whirled away breezily in a mist of heady scent, just as she had arrived. Ben did not watch her go or see Karen looking over her shoulder at him; he just stared at Cassie, almost as if he knew her from a previous life. He shook his head dismissing the notion as Cassie ushered him toward her office.

"I've put some fresh coffee on. We can talk in my office while we have some, what did you call it, 'smoko'?" Cassie smiled nervously and led him into her office. She felt his eyes on her with every step she took. Why did she feel like a schoolgirl just now? *I must snap out of this*. Cassie made a point of sitting on the same side of the desk as Ben, aware of the power plays that happened in offices and keen to work together as a team. She was aware that this wasn't really in his work contract and she badly needed to get him on-side. From a drawer, she pulled out a sketch plan and rolled it on the desk in front of them. "I found some plan drawings of the art centre this morning and copied them freehand. Sorry, they're a bit rough, but I wanted to show you what needs to be done with the walls and the new low voltage lighting I want installed."

"You drew these?" Ben pointed at the plans and leaned sideways in his chair. Cassie's hackles rose at the incredulity in his voice.

"Yes – why not? Women can draw house plans as well as men you know?" Cassie couldn't help sounding annoyed. She needed Ben to do this work but she certainly wasn't going to allow him to patronise her.

"Really? I thought they were pretty good for a girl ..." said Ben with a fake grin. He was feeling uncomfortable, the familiar womanly aroma of Cassie's skin and hair was invading him, but he was not going to be charmed by this enigmatic woman – no way.

"Anyway," Cassie's voice was again calm, attempting to be conciliatory, but she was seething on the inside, "the linings have been ripped off. Apart from being ugly that's a huge amount of display area we've lost."

Ben sat quietly watching Cassie's mouth, barely absorbing her words, intoxicated.

"Then there are the lights we need to properly display the paintings and the toilet drainage. It's blocked and starts backing up after a couple of flushes. We'll be in trouble if a busload of tourists comes in." Cassie barely maintained an even tone. She was hoping he wouldn't hear the pleading in her voice, but as she spoke she saw Ben's gaze was over her shoulder – he was staring at Dumatja's painting. The one she had just sold.

"Ben, did you hear what I said?" exclaimed Cassie, sounding irritated.

"That painting. There's something haunting about it. I don't know why, but it's giving me the creeps." Ben shivered as he stared at the stacks of brown, black and white dots. Cassie quickly turned and then looked back at Ben.

"You too? I've never had a painting do that to me before."

"Alanja and Bulangi told me that the Yolngu art, dance and song always tell a story," said Ben quietly.

"That's George Dumatja's work, I've just sold it," spat Cassie, oblivious of her negative tones. "Do you know Dumatja?" she asked innocently.

"Not really, he doesn't mix much with the other clan leaders. He's a bit on the outer, him and his clan. I think the others are a bit afraid of him. They say he's done bad things."

"I know ... he ... he attacked me yesterday ..."

"What! Attacked you too?" Ben raised his voice – incredulous. "The swine, have you told the police? What happened?" He spoke with concern. Cassie had not heard Ben speak with tenderness before.
Cassie told Ben the story, sparing none of the details about his demands for money and his hands at her throat.

"Mike huh? Mike'll just pay him off. That slime bag won't do anything, he's a carpetbagger."

"Carpet-bagger? What do you mean Ben?"

"That's what they call most of the white CEO's managing aboriginal communities in the Territory. Eight out of ten of them are incompetent, dishonest or both. They couldn't get a job in the real world if their life depended on it."

"Ben, you said something about, 'you too', has he attacked a white woman before? I heard he beats up his wife."
Ben paused, shuffled his boots on the worn lino before answering, "I've just heard rumours, ask Mario or Karen – they've been here longer than I have."

"I already asked Karen – she didn't know anything." Cassie's open palms were raised upwards toward Ben as if in prayer.
Ben shrugged his shoulders and looked to the door.

"Listen, Cassie, I have to go. How about we quickly check out the damage to the wall? Have you got a torch? I'll have a look in the roof space – sneaky buggers those white ants."
Cassie found a torch in one of the desk drawers and led Ben to the middle of the gallery where the dividing wall sat exposed, with the splintered pine framing hanging loosely by the remnant shards. Ben rapidly examined the remains of each stud and then paused under a hatch cover in the ceiling. Cassie quivered when she saw what he did next. He crouched abruptly, his thighs bulging as his shorts rose further up his legs – Cassie's breathing quickened, she unexpectedly felt hot despite the air-conditioning. She watched wide eyed as Ben sprung upwards like a panther. He seemed to pause in the air at the top of his leap, hand neatly pushing the hatch cover

upwards and silently slipping it to one side, before landing silently, still like a big cat.

"I'll just check out the attic," said Ben unaware of her gawking, as he took the torch from Cassie's sweating hand, put it between his teeth and leapt towards the dark hole. Cassie saw a basketballer and a gymnast, not a builder, as she watched Ben propel himself into the opening. After a few moments of footsteps and rattling noises, he called out.

"We're in luck – the little blighters didn't get up into the rafters. Anyway, they're all cypress, the walls are just pine." With a few swift movements, he was back on the floor next to Cassie, the lid closed with athletic precision. "Just for the record, they don't eat cypress."

"What do you think Ben? How quickly could you have it finished? I can help with the plastering and painting," she said hopefully.

"Look Cassie, I don't know that I can do it for a couple of months. I just can't drop everything with the boys training."

"A couple of months? You have to – the Garma Festival is only two months away!" Cassie had raised her voice an octave, forgetting her plan of diplomacy.

"Listen, I don't *have* to do anything! I wasn't hired to do odd jobs in Umbakala. You can always get a contractor across from Darwin," Ben replied. *Was that almost a sneer?*

"Mario said contractors only come out for big jobs or government contracts – anyway, Mike said you'd do it. Please Ben, a quarter of our year's sales come around the Garma Festival!" Cassie was pleading now, having swallowed her pride.

"Then why don't you get your boyfriend to do the work eh? I'm sure you could convince Mario to provide one other service for you!" Ben faced Cassie, both hands on his hips, the veins prominent on his temples and well defined neck muscles.

"How dare you - you ..." Cassie struck out at Ben's cheek with her right hand, but failed to reach the intended target. Ben had her wrist in a strong grip.

"Look – why would I help you anyway? First you smash my boat, now you try to assault me ..."

"Assault you?" Cassie pulled free from his grip and moved forward into his personal space; she repeated, "Assault you? You just insulted me. For your information mister, Mario is not my boyfriend. And at least he was man enough to help a woman when she needed help – not like – like ..."

Without warning, Ben closed the gap between them and silenced her, his lips meeting Cassie's with power and passion. His arms pulled Cassie's trim waist toward him, she could feel her breasts snuggling into his powerful chest – they had already surrendered. Cassie was lost as her arms slowly encircled Ben and she never wanted to be found. She had never yielded to a kiss like this before – her mind, her spirit floated; there was no longer any weight in her body as their tongues met with electric fantasy.

"Oops – sorry – excuse me-ee ..." said Karen, almost singing the words as she felt a pang of jealousy. *That should have been me.* She stood there while Ben and Cassie quickly untangled their bodies, blushes glowing through their tanned faces.

"I- I have to go," was all Ben said as he turned and walked hastily to the door. He saw Rose standing by the door. *Oh great, now everybody knows what an idiot I am.*

"H-hello Rose," he spluttered, barely glancing in her direction as he made his escape into the fresh air.

"Sorry to interrupt Miss Cassie," said Rose deliberately, then paused without making eye contact. "Artists all coming meeting Friday morning. I say ten o'clock."

"Thank you Rose," said Cassie appearing decidedly distracted. "Will Dumatja be there as well?"

"He say he come Miss. He say he got money from Mike – no need worry no more Miss Cassie."

A wave of relief came over Cassie on learning this news.

"Rose, Karen, can we just have a quick meeting now please? I'd like to go over Friday's meeting with the two of you. It would be good to go over things you've talked about in past meetings. We could start planning for the Garma Festival as well."

"Sure boss," said Karen, again her chirpy self. Cassie could not tell if this was a facade. She knew Karen was after Ben and now she had found the two of them kissing. *Kissing? That was beyond kissing,* recounted Cassie as she led Rose and Karen into her office. She forced the memory to the back of her mind. After all, she was here to do a job, the best job she could, not have an affair with a surly itinerant builder with a fancy boat. Boat? That reminded Cassie to put a memo into her diary to see Mario about ordering some materials to repair Ben's boat. She would honour her obligations in spite of the type of man Ben was.

After the meeting, Cassie was buoyant, encouraged with the information gathered from Rose and Karen. There were three women artists who had been organising Garma displays in a hired marquee for the past four years and one of them was Rose. Cassie had learnt to her relief, that Dumatja would not be involved in their display, as he normally was one of the lead dancers in the dance competition between the region's communities. It was agreed that Karen would stay behind at the Art Centre and manage the sales from the tourist overflow. As she charted her plans and timetable on her wall planner, there was still the one imperative task. The repair to the art centre. Apart from that Cassie was gaining back her old confidence and optimism. She remembered her dad's favourite quotes to her when she was a little girl, 'There's no such word as can't.'

Just as Cassie was about to head out to the main office to talk to Mike, a smiling face popped around the door of her office.

"Hi gorgeous, I was just passing and thought I'd drop in," beamed Mario. Before Cassie could respond he asked, "Hey is that coffee for important people or can anyone have some?"

Cassie smiled back; somehow Mario was a welcome relief from the events of the morning.

"Sure thing Mario, but don't you have barnacles to scrape or rigging to replace, or something?"

"I'd like to scrape *your* barnacles, darling," he retorted with a wink. Cassie ignored the double entendre and replied,

"No thanks Mario, I had my bottom scraped in Fiji. There was a nice man in the Suva Yacht Club – even gave me a good deal on the antifoul paint." She winked back at him, happy to have some light hearted conversation for a change. Cassie poured Mario a cup of coffee and passed some biscuits, still lying on the plate, untouched from Ben's visit. Mario, still smiling, added,

"Look Cassie, I'm still worried about Dumatja – I'll be happy to stay the night again if you like."

"I don't think that will be necessary Mario, Rose told me that Mike already paid Dumatja."

"At any rate, he still might have it in for you Cassie and look; you'll be doing me a favour. I've had weeks of having awful dinners on my own, it's just good talkin' with ya Cassie."

"Okay Mario," laughed Cassie, "One more night then – just in case. But I'm meeting with the artists, including Dumatja on Friday, so I'm hoping to have it all sorted after that."

"Right – bewdy - I'll see you at six!" he leapt to his feet, "Gotta scrape some more barnacles off another bottom!"

"And remember? No funny business!" said Cassie sternly.

"I don't know what you mean?" said Mario feigning hurtfulness. "See you later alligator!" as he dashed out of the art centre.

Time to see Mike, thought Cassie as she tidied her planning documents and slipped the paperwork into the filing cabinet. She stopped when her desk was neat again, only her diary left open at today's page. As she grabbed a notebook and pen, ready to go up to the council office, Cassie spotted a folded, half crumbled piece of paper on the floor. It was ruled and had neat hand printing on it in black ink. She picked it up and started to read,

"Angelic face – tropical dream
My heart cracked apart
Ripe nut full of cream.
Her eyes sated smart
Her voice it would seem
Tolls loud iron darts
Steel bells on my beam."

Hand shaking, Cassie re-read the verse two more times, *Mario – he must have dropped this on the floor. Did he mean for me to find it? Wow, talk about still waters.* Cassie carefully folded it and tucked the paper in the back of her diary. *Was this about love? Was this about me?* She mentally shook herself back to reality, back to her reality of sorting out this building matter with Mike. *This is madness; one man kisses me like Don Juan and another writes love poetry. I can't believe this – this just can't be happening.*

The sky was blue again and Cassie noted that the trade winds were still blowing, rattling the gum leaves like playing cards being flicked by a thousand card players. As she approached the council offices, she saw Mike's car parked in front along with a few scruffy white trucks and four wheel drives. Cassie reminded herself to visit the store before heading home to buy more fresh produce – her temporary larder needed serious replenishment and she needed to feed Mario. This time she was able to push the door open without operating the security lock; there was a crushed soft drink can wedged neatly in the door. The cool air welcomed her inside where two small Yolngu girls were sitting on the floor playing with their dolls. They acknowledged Cassie with four bright eyes as she stepped past, then immediately resumed their game. Behind the reception counter were three Yolngu women chatting in their own language. The phone was ringing but no one moved to answer. As she walked toward Mike's office, Cassie noted that all three women glanced briefly in her direction but made no eye contact or attempt to find out her business. *Not a great way to manage a business*, she thought caustically. The phone was still ringing as Cassie found Mike's door. It was open and she saw Mike at the same time that he saw her. He was looking at something that appeared to be a glossy brochure, which he quickly slid into his top drawer when he saw Cassie.

"Come in, come in," said Mike as he stood up to greet her. He wasn't wearing a tie today, just a short sleeved striped shirt stained with sweat circles under his arms like two soft plates. A triangle of white singlet appeared just above his belt, squeezed by his soft belly.

"How are you Cassie? What's happening down at the art centre then? Sold any work? Settling in okay?"

Cassie felt repulsed by his fawning manner and disbelieving that he did not ask how she was after the Dumatja attack. Despite her fury, she fully intended to keep this business-like as she sat upright in the visitor's chair, her notebook propped neatly in her lap. "I need to discuss some important issues with you Mike. Firstly there's the matter of Dumatja. I heard that you paid him some money."

"Yes, yes, that's all taken care of. Dumatja came into my office yesterday and I gave him an advance on his art work. I told you I'd sort it out."

"You gave him an advance?" echoed Cassie. "Is that normal Mike? I mean how are you going to account for that payment?"

"Well – er – yes, you see, we'll just charge that to 'Artist's Payments' in your cost of sales. Quite simple really."

"Hang on a minute," Cassie almost spluttered, "If you just give him money whenever he asks for it, how can we match that to his sales?"

"Er – yes, good point. Look, you must know that we, er, do things differently around here. Arnhem Land is like another world; Yolngu, *these* people think differently to us ..."

"That's fine Mike, but didn't you tell me the art centre was having financial difficulties?"

"Yes - but .."

"Didn't you tell me I was responsible for making it profitable? So how can I be responsible if you hand out money to someone who holds you to ransom?"

"Hang on a minute, Miss Greenway. I was just solving *your* problem with Dumatja – I was protecting *you*!"

"No wonder the art centre's losing money – we're supposed to have a policy of paying artists only after we sell their works!" retorted Cassie, her voice raised in annoyance. A sense of frustration had risen within her – any confidence she expected in Mike as a boss was no longer there.

"Now Cassie, be reasonable, I know the way to handle these people – you have to trust me on this." His finger tugged at his shirt collar in discomfort as he spoke.

"Sorry Mike, but I've been comparing your computer sales figures with our records and they just don't seem to add up. Tell me, how can I be held responsible as a manager if all the sales aren't recorded? Or worse still – money goes missing?"

"Now look here young lady, what exactly are you accusing me of?" Mike's face was white with fury, a vein had popped up on his temple – it wasn't there a minute ago.

"I'm *not* accusing you of anything. Can't you see *my* point of view? How can I be held accountable for the finances?"

"Look, I'll see what we can do to sort this out – just leave it with me. I'll have a word with Janice the book-keeper. Just the same, we'll have to terminate this little meeting, I'm very busy, I'm about to fly out to Darwin on business - council business. We can talk more about this when I get back but next time perhaps you could make an appointment." The vein on the side of his head had subsided and his mouth widened as if trying to smile.

"One more thing before you go, Mike if you could possibly make the time. Ben says he can't do the work in the next two months. The toilet's blocked, Garma is coming, how can I do my job properly if the infrastructure's not right?"

"Yes, yes – I'll have another chat to Ben when I get back, just leave it all with me – we'll get it sorted for you. Now if there's nothing else?" he raised his eyebrows and stood up, attempting to close the meeting.

"Just one final thing – will I be safe in my own bed at night?"

Cassie spent the afternoon in the gallery burning off nervous energy, rearranging exhibits, dusting cobwebs and familiarising herself with the works and the artist's styles. The learning would have been much more fun if it hadn't been for the frustrations of the day. She kept re-playing the drama that happened with Ben, especially *that* kiss. *How dare he insinuate that Mario and I were, were...* Cassie fought to remain composed but her mind and body kept straying back to that moment when Ben's lips had electrified her body in a way she had dreamed possible. Why hadn't she pushed him away? Unable to forgive herself, Cassie pondered her body's betrayal and now her mind's inability to deal with this. Why? She wondered why she was losing control of her life. Cassie sensed something powerful, perhaps something spiritual, an aura that enveloped her that she wasn't able to escape. It was like being trapped in a dream and she wanted to wake up, to be normal again. She sensed the evil, but wanted the good. She hoped something or someone would take her to the good – she prayed quietly – for the good.

In the meantime, Karen had decided to deliberately avoid Cassie if she could. She was not able to forget *that* kiss either. *Cassie doesn't even like Ben – why did she let him kiss her? Well, I'm not giving up. I know he likes me – I just know it!* Karen looked again at Ben's hat in her desk drawer. She had found it on the wood carving where Ben had placed it before leaping into the attic. Taking it out of its hiding place, Karen looked around to check if Cassie was watching. Satisfied Cassie was still in the galleries; Karen put her face into the hat and breathed in deeply. He smelled just fine – she imagined how pleasant his moulded bicep might smell as she snuggled into the crook of his arm. She quickly snapped out of her daydream when she heard footsteps behind her. As she slammed the hat back into her drawer, Karen hoped that Cassie hadn't seen it – she was hatching plans for that hat.

Ben heaved off his work boots and threw them across the boat toward the v-berth. He slid his feet across the carpeted floor, enjoying the coarse massage and freedom from the prison of the steel caps. One of his usual one pot dinners was already in the pressure cooker as he reached across to the navigation table drawer and carefully pulled out a framed picture. He stared at the photo as he lay down, then kissed the glass. *"I'm sorry my darling – I don't know why it has to be this way – I'm sorry."* He put the picture face down on his chest and closed his eyes, hoping for some peace. His mind was racing with the images from today. He regretted his feelings, his desires. *Why did I lose control? I don't grab women and kiss them? I don't do that.* He lifted his head, eyes open, as he felt the boat suddenly rock to one side.

"Hello-o? Are you there Ben?" He sighed, it was Karen – he didn't want company tonight. Ben had already told Garrawarra that he wouldn't be coming to North beach tonight – he had said he needed to do things on the boat. It wasn't a lie – he needed to cook dinner and to forget about today, that was all.

"Come on down Karen." Ben's voice was weary, drained of enthusiasm. He carefully replaced the picture in the drawer just before Karen stepped down into the cabin.

"Sorry to barge in on you Ben, but I brought you this ..." she said brightly, hopefully as she held out his hat, "And this?" as she raised a brown paper bag in the shape of a bottle.

"Thanks, I wondered where that had disappeared to," lied Ben, knowing full well he had left it at the art centre, but there was no way he was going back to get it, after his little exhibition. He had lots of other hats.

"You'd better stay for dinner then, I've got enough for two – is that wine?" reluctantly he invited her to join him.

"Yep it's a Barossa Valley Merlot – is that okay?"

"My favourite. I hope you don't mind curried fish and rice?"

Karen chatted most of the time while they were eating. Ben kept nodding encouragingly, secretly grateful for this interruption; Karen had taken his mind off his burden. When they had finished both the food and the wine, Karen put one foot up on the settee, her sarong slipping open to expose her endless legs spread provocatively. Ben caught a glimpse of white panties, but immediately looked away – he wouldn't be tempted – again. Then unexpectedly, came Karen's invitation.

"Ben, I'm going out on Saturday with some of the Yolngu artists. We're off to the bush to get grasses and paperbark 'n stuff. Would you like to come? We could use a big strong bloke like you to rip those slabs of bark off the trees – we might have a picnic as well?"

Almost too quickly, Ben replied,

"Sorry Karen, I should be doing things on my boat." He nodded over to the gaping hole in the hull, "Your boss did that." Karen changed the subject, not wanting to talk about Cassie; after all, she was competition.

"Oh, well, if you change your mind... Ben, it's dark and late and with Dumatja on the warpath – do you mind if I camp on your boat tonight – promise I won't be any trouble."

Ben shook his head and paused, he didn't want to hurt her feelings or start something else he might regret. He never believed in casual sex - he wasn't going to start now. He reached for fresh socks and his boots,

"Come on, I'll walk you home – I just want a night on my own tonight."

Karen sat petulantly with her arms folded, legs crossed, while Ben put on his boots. They walked up the hill in silence. It was another moonlit night, as they passed the art centre, then up to Cassie's house on the way to the village where Karen lived. Ben could see two people on Cassie's verandah. The lights were off in the house and he heard a man and a woman's voice – then laughter. Karen smiled to herself, then added pointedly,

"Looks like Mario's stayin' the night again eh?"

Ben said nothing, but looked straight ahead – jealous bile rising in his gut again.

It wasn't long before they arrived at the nurse's quarters where Karen was billeted.

"Thanks for that great dinner Ben. Are you sure ya won't change your mind about Saturday?" she asked hopefully.

"You know, I might just take you up on that Karen. What time are we leaving?

5   Meeting Dumatja Again

Cassie arrived home that evening, sweating profusely and heavy laden with groceries. She imagined how good it would have been to drive home in the air-conditioned art centre troop carrier, but had let Karen borrow it for the weekend. Karen had arranged to take some of the artists out to gather bush materials and had invited Cassie to come along. Cassie was tempted but had declined, promising to go next time. This weekend she had to organise materials to fix Ben's boat and clean and do some service work on her own boat. The rudder could wait, until she was desperate for a sail, but she couldn't neglect Serendipity, her beautiful '70's Californian classic that had brought her safely here. For a moment she daydreamed about sailing further west, to Bali, then on to Thailand, but her funds were low. She knew there was no escape from Umbakala for a while and her manager's salary was more than adequate to top up her bank account. Cassie was confident her parents would come to the rescue if the worse came to the worse. They were always offering to help with money when Cassie was at college, but Cassie was too stubborn, too independent to accept their help. *My parents!* She remembered they did not know she had arrived in Australia safely – feeling guilty that she had been too busy with work and all the crazy stuff going on in her life ever since she got here she decided she must ring them today. It was going to be hard keeping things back from them but she *couldn't* tell them everything, they would be so relieved to hear she was safe in Australia that it was just too cruel to tell them that she'd been attacked. She would just have to say that all was well and that she was enjoying the people and the cultural learning. Cassie practiced her imaginary chat to her mom and dad, vowing to tell them as much truth as possible, she would just spare them some of the detail- after all, Mario and Rose were nice and the art was fantastic. They could not cope with the stories about Ben and Mike, let alone Dumatja. They just didn't need to know. Anyway, she was 31, old enough to have some secrets from her parents.

Just before dark, Cassie heard urgent, heavy footsteps bounding up her front wooden steps. The whole house shook slightly – it was mounted on steel poles which appeared to be flimsy, but Mario had assured her that the house had been built after Cyclone Tracy had devastated Darwin. He explained to her that there had been strict cyclone building codes ever since and her house was built to withstand cyclonic winds.

"Come in Mario, dinner won't be long."

"Ta daaa!" Mario entered dramatically, arms outstretched with a bottle of beer in each hand. A bag of corn chips he had tucked under an arm fell to the floor. "Oops, we'll have to throw them away now!" he said mockingly, continuing the drama.

Cassie laughed as she pummelled carrots against a hand grater.

"Oh, I don't know. I might have to send you to the store to buy another bag. Oops, forgot! It shuts at five so I think we'll just *have* to eat them even if they are crushed. There's a bowl in the top cupboard over there, just pop the chips in there – and yes, while you're at it, I'd love a beer, it's been one helluva day."

Mario talked almost non-stop about the sixty foot ketch which had anchored in the main harbour while Cassie pumped him for information. Mario had met the English sailors when he went to have lunch at the yacht club so he had plenty to tell her. He also spoke about his friends who worked at the bauxite plant who he met up with at least once a week.

"I bought some leg ham and made up a fresh salad Mario, I hope that's okay?"

"Beaudy, thanks Cassie," said Mario as he started devouring the meat like a starving peasant.

Such a paradox ... works with his hands yet writes poetry; eats like a pig but cares for women – well sort of, Cassie mused.

While Mario was eating, Cassie told him about her meeting with Mike and about Ben not being able to fix up the art centre for two months. She told him everything but didn't mention *that* kiss. Cassie blushed as she relived the moment of her surprised surrender. She looked at Mario's lips, glistening and moist from the ham fat he had eaten carelessly – they were full blooded Italian lips. *How many women have they kissed? What would it be like kissing Mario?*

While Cassie finished her meal, Mario talked more about himself, the music he liked, the TV shows he liked to watch. There was no mention of poetry. She stared at his Roman face, the aquiline nose, the statuesque bone structure. Maybe she would sculpt him some day – if she ever found time for her own pleasures.

"Why don't we finish the beer and chips on the verandah Mario?"

He looked surprised at this offer, but eagerly accepted. There was only an outdoor sofa suspended on a frame by chains. This was all going better that he had expected. *Maybe tonight I'll get lucky?* He thought as he looked longingly at Cassie's gorgeous round bottom, wiggling and jiggling ever so slightly as she receded into the kitchen with the dinner plates.

Cassie sat deliberately in one of the corners of the sofa but somehow in the space of chatting for an hour and a half, Mario had managed to edge himself closer. His knee was now touching Cassie's thigh. She felt a sudden shortness of breath, her heart beating faster in her chest – she could see the lips on Mario's face moving but could not concentrate on the words. She felt her own animal urges coming to the surface again. The beer must have relaxed her because one way or another Mario had snaked one arm around Cassie's shoulders and the other rested tenderly on her thigh. His eyes were gentle, soft and half closed – bedroom eyes, coming closer....

"No, Mario, no, we mustn't...," she pushed him away...

"Aw, come on Cassie, you know you want it as much as I do – I mean, you're not a virgin are you?" he pulled back; feigning horror in his expression, as if virginity was a crime or at the very least a rare disease like leprosy where sufferers were to be shunned or treated as outcasts.

"Mario, that's none of your business!" She paused, searching for words as she looked out into the blackness. There were frogs competing with a traditional singer and some duller rap music – all oozing out of the night that she felt closing in on her. Cassie took a deliberate sip of beer; it was only her second glass.

"Look - I like you Mario – I feel safe with you, and you are very handsome you know – but ..." She hadn't finished the sentence when Mario butted in.

"No buts Cassie, it's not healthy to go without sex. It's like eating and drinking – like breathing!"

Cassie stood up and made her way to the edge of the balcony. She turned and leaned back, tousled hair cascading over her shoulders, elbows on the top rail. She looked at Mario, a Mona Lisa smile on her face.

"What about love?"

It was Mario who didn't answer straight away. He thought about Rhonda as he stared into the night, his smile growing wistful as he cradled his beer with both hands.

"I was in love once."

"Only once?" asked Cassie.

"Not counting stupid crushes ya get when you're a kid. Yeah, I thought the sun shone out of Rhonda's – well, you know."

"No I don't Mario; I don't think I've ever really been in love. There was James of course, but he was just comfortable, convenient. In the end, I'm not sure if I ever really loved him at all."

"I don't believe in love any more. I mean, what's the point? You give your heart to someone then she just stomps on it, rips your guts out and what have you got left to show for it? Nothin' but empty guts and a hole in your chest!"

They both laughed at Mario's outburst.

"I think it's time I went to bed Mario – *alone!*" Cassie insisted but with a smile on her face, "Remember, I've got a big day tomorrow. I get to meet Dumatja again."

When Cassie awoke, the sun was already beaming in through her bedroom window and Mario had already gone. This time there was no breakfast made, no note left behind. *If he can write poetry, I would have thought he'd have written a note?* Scoffing her muesli, Cassie projected her thoughts toward the meeting with the artists. She had calculated they needed more stock for the Garma festival – she had made her calculations on the previous year's sales. How would she motivate them? In her mind she kept skirting around Dumatja. Cassie couldn't face even thinking about what he might say, what he might do? How would she feel – frightened? *I must stay calm, focussed.* She breathed deeply and drained the last gulp of coffee before heading out to work.

Karen was already at the art centre putting out cups on a table she had set up in the main gallery. A pitcher of orange cordial stood in the middle of the table, covered in a muslin cloth which had shells sewn round the edges to hold it down. Three plates of biscuits were scattered haphazardly, almost an artistic arrangement in itself.

"Sorry I'm late Karen, I slept in. You must think I'm a hypocrite."

"Oh, I'm sure you had a *very* good reason not to get a lot of sleep last night Cassie." Karen winked as she spoke. The implication was not missed by Cassie but she ignored the remark, the wink and commented instead on the meeting arrangements.

"Well done Karen. So traditionally we all sit on the floor, the mats that is, while we talk?"

"Yep and I got the bikkies out of petty cash like we always do."

"That's right, Mike told me about that. He said if you want to get Yolngu to come to a meeting, put on food! He also said not to expect them to come at a set time. Is that right?" Cassie asked in her Californian twang, but already was adding an Australian inflection to the end of her sentences.

"Yeah, that's all true. Someone'll come on time, then dribs and drabs, but mostly they should be all here by eleven. You can start the meeting proper then."

At nine thirty Rose arrived with three other Yolngu artists, all women.

"This Mary Djalanga, Sarah Murutji and Emily Datjun," said Rose, introducing three shy ladies, all with greying hair, brightly coloured skirts and dusty bare feet.

"Hello ladies – Namirri!" Cassie smiled, shaking each hand in turn as they giggled and returned smiles.

"Great, I see you've brought some art works!" Cassie looked across at the rolled up paintings and handful of ornate baskets. "Please, please, put them out on the table, let's have a look." Cassie excitedly fussed over the works, eager to hear the stories behind the art.

"This one settlement story. Story of two sisters who came by boat – Yolngu people all from these sisters," explained Mary Djalanga. She was tall and slender, her hands moved gracefully like brown doves swooping down to the work and fluttering around in the air till the story was told. Cassie could see how pleased they were at her obvious enjoyment and appreciation of their works. Cassie looked across to the noise of the front door opening again with some trepidation. Her fingers massaged her temples. It was four more women, two of them carrying paintings, one a large woven mat. Rose in her quiet way introduced them to Cassie who welcomed them warmly and fussed over their art. Only one of the young women had difficulty talking in English, the older ones had all gone to school in the days of the missionaries and spoke well. Cassie already knew that English was often a sixth language for the Yolngu. They spoke their own plus five other dialects before even needing or learning English. Cassie was impressed with their work and despite her anxiety about Dumatja, enjoyed their company. The informal gathering was much like when she was at art school back in the States. They were all artists, all with a common interest as they freely discussed techniques and processes and materials and what drove or motivated their works. Cassie experienced a truly exhilarating moment as she moved comfortably among the women. The talk turned to Garma and songs and dance. Cassie felt cocooned by the aura of love and fellowship extended by these beautiful women. At last she felt a sense of belonging, a sense at having arrived at the right place at the right time in her life. Then the spell was broken. Cassie held her breath as the door opened. The room hushed. Women stood still as if a predator eagle had swooped over a flock of hens. Cassie felt all eyes on her. Dumatja strode into the room followed by four Yolngu men, faces stern and serious. The strong crease lines in his taut black face showed no emotion. He walked straight up to Cassie, made no eye contact, but stood beside her looking out over the small group.

"We meet now – I am George Dumatja," his voice deep and resonant, gravelly from years of smoking, yet commanding respect or was it fear? He moved over to one of the large mats and sat down cross-legged beckoning everyone else to sit. Cassie sat in the circle that had formed between Karen and Rose. She didn't notice the slight tremble in Karen's hands, the paling of her cheeks or the extra perspiration on her palms; Karen had her own demons rising to the surface.

"We welcome Miss Cassie Greenway. New art centre manager.

Miss Cassie come from California. My cousin sell yidaki there – visit 2 times," he looked across to Cassie as if waiting for a response. Cassie was confused, uncertain, pausing before responding, hoping her voice would not quaver or reveal her fear of this man.

"Thank you for your welcome Mr Dumatja. Please – please all of you, call me Cassie. And you sir? What would you like me to call you?" asked Casssie, politely, her eyes steely and focused, only the slight tremor in her voice belying her true emotions.

"Dumatja – jus' Dumatja."

"Very well – Dumatja. I understand you are a clan leader and have some leadership with artists? Is that right?"

"Yo, me clan leader – and art centre *my* clan business. I manage art centre three year past."

"Thank you Dumatja, I'll be glad to have your valuable experience. Now if everyone is ready, I will begin. There are a number of topics I feel we need to talk about. There's the Garma Festival, repairs to the building, some marketing ideas and of course the finances." There was a fragile sense of peace as the meeting started without conflict.

For the next twenty minutes, Cassie talked about the arrangements for the festival and confirmed the roles each of the artists would have. Rose translated into Yolngu language to make sure that everyone understood. The air was tense – no one moved – Cassie did nearly all of the talking but no one questioned her authority and she knew she already had the respect from the women. Everyone listened as Cassie talked about her frustrations with the delays to the building repairs and told them about Mike's latest promise to look for a contractor from Darwin who would be able to do the all-important work before Garma.

"Are there any questions?" asked Cassie as she looked around the circle, more confident now that she had covered all the agenda points. Soon the meeting would be over but she still had to deal with the most difficult topic.

"Perhaps the most important thing we need to talk about is the finance," she started.

"You mean – money story?" Dumatja raised his heavy eyebrows, like lifting a black velvet curtain from his casket eyes.

"Y-yes, the money story, if you like. When I first arrived Mike Britliff told me that the art centre was in a bad way. There just isn't enough money. He told me we needed to sell many paintings so we can fix things and pay you more." Cassie was trying very hard not to sound patronising, unsure of how her language sounded, unsure of how much understanding Yolngu had of Western marketing systems and even more unsure of how Dumatja might react when talking about money. She didn't have long to wait. Dumatja's eyes became like slits – Cassie could feel the blackness and evil glaring from the narrow openings.

"There's always money," his voice was now raised. "Yolngu custom to share. Yolngu warrior race; Yolngu proud race we live here before money story come – our dreamtime, our stories, our songs; long before white man come. You white fella work for us – we NEED money, you GIVE money – that clan way, Yolngu way," he paused after his dramatic emotional speech. Cassie deliberated, she was scared. *Mustn't show my fear. I don't know what he's talking about. How can I answer this?*

"I understand – I respect your culture, your people, but you must understand. The white fella money story is different to the Yolngu way," she pleaded. It hadn't gone unnoticed, Dumatja had seen her weakness. To Dumatja women were weak, only he was strong.

"No more this Yapa!' Dumatja rose to his full height and pointed a long bony finger straight at Cassie. Cassie gulped and feared the worse. Her hands went to her neck feeling the bruises that showed their last encounter. She looked at Rose and Karen, now, seeking help. If he attacked her here and now, no one would help her, he seemed to have some sort of power over them all. *He's going to kill me and no one's going to lift a finger*, was her panicking thought.

"You work Yolngu way Miss Cassie! You do money business clan way – my way!" He thumped his chest, it echoed like the sound of an axe on a hollow log. She sat there, petrified, unable to move as Dumatja turned abruptly and spoke rapidly in Yolngu. The men got up and left with him, followed by the women, then Cassie was left alone with Karen and Rose. She was heartened as some of the women gave her discreet smiles as they passed. There was some hope, a small candle in a blazing fire, a small glow to keep her optimism and hope alight.

The glow from the clock by the bed illuminated the room the first time Cassie woke. *Two am. Only two?* She'd been waiting a long time for sleep that night and couldn't believe she'd only managed a meagre hour. She sat up and kneaded her feather pillow into another new shape, like a misshapen muffin. She untangled the sheet from her restless legs and let it settle, a cool cloud on a hot valley. She sipped on a glass of water, hoping to wash away images of Dumatja's warrior face from her mind. Her eyes searched again the dark shadows of her room. Closing her eyes, Cassie forced a reflection of tropical islands she had visited in the pacific. *Penrhyn – perfect Penrhyn.* She visualised the vivid blue coral atoll as Serendipity had motored into the lagoon past the smiling natives paddling in their traditional wooden canoes. She remembered the warmth of the welcome, the gifts of tropical fruits they had given her. She had taken children's clothes and soaps to share with the women. Before leaving San Francisco she had Googled Penrhyn and read on a site, that the population of 400 was 60% Christian and 40% Catholic.... she smiled as her eyes grew heavy, still amused by that web page. Calmed by her memories she finally slept.

It was six when Cassie woke. Stifling two yawns, she knew it was pointless trying to sleep any more. Coffee, toast and peanut butter – then absently she looked around for Mario, suddenly realising that this was her first night alone in the house. Perhaps it was that meeting that haunted her all night? Perhaps Dumatja had already cursed her? *No way! I don't believe in that hocus pocus – just the power of suggestion, that's all. Something that only affects weak minds – not me.*

Cassie put on her work shorts, a paint stained t-shirt and a battered Seventy Sixers cap. Well-worn joggers completed her practical outfit for working on the boat. She hoped no Yolngu men would see her on the way to the dock. Shorts may be taboo but there was no way she could work on the boat in a skirt. There were no homes between her house and the water, so she was reasonable confident that she would not be seen. There was no music this early, just morning bird songs and the ever blue sky fell upon Cassie walking down the snake like path. Ahead of her, she heard a smooth noise slither through in the leaves, moving away from the path. Not scared, but cautious, she warily peered through the undergrowth looking for the creature. *Taipan, Death Adder, Brown snake?* They could all kill within minutes. *Mustn't annoy them.* Her tension eased, ironically diverted from her troubles by the presence of deadly snakes.

Cassie approached her boat in the dock, much more relaxed than she had been for the past twenty four hours. Serendipity was glowing in the morning light; there was not a ripple on the water. All was still - except for two bare feet waggling on the wall of the cockpit of Ben's boat. He had a mug in his hand and a serene far-away look in his eyes. Cassie tried to suppress the memory of their last encounter of, Ben's strong arms around her, his lips hungrily exploring hers. She had little success - he was wearing a white t-shirt that clung to the strong ripples of his chest and arms. Cassie stared for a moment longer than she should have whilst thinking. *I must talk to him – I must be civil.*

"Good morning Ben, I think we need to talk." Cassie was pleased the way that came out – cool, professional - no emotion. She focussed on his eyes, not letting her gaze stray down to the blond hairs on his forearms or the glorious tanned legs. Her cheeks burned.

"Thought maybe I said too much yesterday?" Ben's eyes moved quickly from her face down to her feet and back again - too quick to be considered undressing. *She's even beautiful in her work gear. Stay calm boy – don't let her get to you again.*

"As I remember, you didn't exactly do much talking ..."

"I'm sorry about that. Don't know what came over me – that's what happens when a girl gets too close to an angry lion." Ben smiled, trying hard to lighten the mood and to hide his raging emotions. This woman by her very presence made him angry, made him happy, made him – want her. *No, not now – not ever. Besides, she's Mario's girl.*

"Sort of like, Goldilocks meets the lion on the yellow Brick Road?"

"Touché Goldilocks – round one to you! Are we going to keep talking fairy tales on carousels, or do we get to the Grimm's tale where the big bad girl wolf smashes the house of the innocent little piggy?" His grin was contagious. Cassie relaxed and smiled back, one hand was on her hip, now tilted in a provocative manner. The shape and seductive curve of hip, thigh and breast in tight T-shirt did not go unnoticed by Ben.

"Round two to you Ben. Why don't we call it even and talk about how I'm going to fix your boat? Sorry, I mean how this big bad girl wolf puts back together the helpless little piggy's house?"

"Two to one! Or is that 30-15? Not much of a tennis player myself – is it still my serve?" Cassie wanted to laugh, but couldn't bring herself to give Ben the satisfaction that she might find him amusing. He could still explode at any minute – every time they had met he had somehow become angry. She just wasn't sure how to handle him and then there was *that* kiss.

"No, no; still your serve, unless you'd like to simply forfeit the match?"

"This isn't getting us anywhere," said Ben mockingly. "We could settle this with a little arm wrestle – winner takes all?"

Cassie surprised Ben when she stepped over boldly to the edge of the wharf, leaned over; her body suspended above the water and assumed the arm wrestling position on the edge of Ben's boat.

"Okay fella – let's go – winner takes all!"

There was a momentary look of astonishment in Ben's eyes, round like saucers. He stared into Cassie's blue eyes. *Hmm*, he thought, b*rown hair and blue eyes, so lovely.*

Neither one blinked. Cassie took the strain, her left hand gripped the rub rail for extra leverage – she pushed; not with all her might, she knew this was not an even fight. This was a test for Ben. *What sort of a man is he? Will he make me look a weakling? Will he hurt me to get even? Will he, will he – kiss me?* The colour rose from her neck up as she realised how much she wanted to feel his touch again. Even this was enticing as she felt her small hand encircled in the strong grip of his palm. She hoped Ben wouldn't notice the shortness of her breath. *Those handsome latté eyes – he's looking straight into my soul.* She saw love, pain and danger. *Careful girl, he's dangerous.*

Ben held her hand, enjoying the softness of the petite fingers. He could feel every inch of flesh, could feel the small callouses on the inside of her fingers, from her months of sailing. Sailors' callouses – callouses of a kindred spirit, the spirit of the sea he was bound to, devoted his life to. It seemed like an hour, but it was less than a minute. Ben slowly allowed his arm to be pushed backwards. He pretended to grimace. He pretended he was in pain, clutching his bicep as Cassie completed the final push of his hand onto the deck. She rose to her feet, both hands in the air, clenched fists, shaking her hips as she did in her high school cheer leader days.

"Yay! USA One – Australia nil! Headline – Goldilocks beats lion in thrilling contest Down Under!" She plonked herself down on the dock again, a bit more of her tanned thigh showing. It was now Ben who was admiring lovely legs. Cassie did not notice Ben's stare, she was still cheering herself.

They were both laughing when the white troop carrier pulled up at the end of the dock. Karen was at the wheel, the passenger seat empty but the back full of the Yolngu artists. As she heard the laughter she switched off the engine and her face turned grim. Ben and Cassie looked across, their heads turning as one.

The two timing bitch, thought Karen. *She's got Mario and now she's after Ben. Well, he's mine – she can't have him – he's mine.* Karen composed herself and fixed a smile on her face before climbing out and walking over to Cassie and Ben.

"Hi Ben, ya ready to go?"

"Yep. I'll just put my boots on Karen. Cassie and I are just about done here anyway." Karen could see embarrassment in both their faces. *What have they been up to?*

"Before you go Ben, I hope you don't mind. I spoke to Mario about materials to fix your boat. He's ordering the special resin recommended for her so I can make a start on the repair next weekend. Is that okay?"

"Mario? Yeah - sure – whatever Cassie." Ben sounded offhand. The magic was gone. Cassie wondered which was the 'real Ben'. The moody perfectionist, angry about his boat who had seized her; or the fun, relaxed, friendly guy who was trying to help the Yolngu. Was he high maintenance, an emotional roller coaster ride? Or was it just her, was she the one on the emotional roller coaster?

"Have fun Karen. Hope you get plenty of materials." Cassie gave a cheery wave to the smiling women in the troop carrier. They waved back with big grins. It pleased Cassie; at least here there were easy relationships, simple friendships – artist to artist, uncomplicated, not like with Ben or Karen. *Fix Ben's boat then spend more time with the Yolngu artists,* she decided. *Forget about men and definitely forget about* that *kiss.* She would plunge herself in the Yolngu culture. She did not need men – didn't need love. Not now anyway.

6   Yolngu Barbeque

Cassie watched the troopy drive along the track behind the beach before disappearing into the scrub and gum trees on the road leading to the village. She was desperate to explore the countryside with her new friends, gather art materials with them and maybe even learn about their bush tucker, traditional foods. There would be plenty of time for that in the future she hoped. Trying to convince herself she did not care, Cassie pondered the image of Karen's hand stroking Ben's arm as she'd walked with him to the vehicle. She wondered if Karen would try to seduce Ben. Wrestling again with her emotions she wondered what had just happened between her and Ben? For that brief moment she had enjoyed Ben's company as a friend. She had been able to drop her guard, laugh and be silly with him, so why had he changed all of a sudden? Was he just another ladies man like Mario appeared to be? To Cassie they were both complex, both oozing masculine sexuality, both dragging behind some luggage of pain. Why couldn't they be simple? At least Mario was more transparent – he was still hurting after Rhonda ran off. But Ben? What was his problem? What did he want out of life? From her?

After opening all the hatches to air the boat and putting her things inside, Cassie made her way along the shore to Mario's boatyard, hoping he would be there on a Saturday morning. His weather-beaten four wheel drive utility was parked outside. There were fishing rods tied to the roof. She knocked on the door. It opened quickly and in front of her was a tangle of black, like mohair carpet on polished timber. Mario was wearing a pair of tight work shorts and nothing else. He scratched the hair on his brawny chest, smiled broadly and invited her inside.

"It's not a social call," Cassie offered, not knowing where to look – his bronzed torso unnerved her. "Just wanted to confirm those materials for Ben's boat. Will they get here by next Saturday?"

"They'll be here on Tuesday's barge Cassie – no worries. My supplier's very reliable – just like me!"

"You?"

"Yep, you can always count on me – for a kiss!" He leaned in towards Cassie, lips puckered, still smiling.

"That's not exactly my key definition of *reliable*." *Cassie* laughed and put up both hands like stop signals to thwart any forward progress. Mario put a fist over his heart and the back of his other hand to his forehead and rolled his eyes melodramatically.

"Ouch, that hurt Cassie. Anyway, when you want the best; you know where to come."

"Thanks Mario. I'll keep that in mind. So tell me, what do you usually do on a weekend?"

"I usually go fishing – and when I'm not fishing, I'm fishing! Going out to the reef with some miner mates today. Hey, do you want to come? We've got lots of beer?"

"No thanks Mario, I've got maintenance to do on Serendipity this weekend."

"Maybe next weekend?"

"Not for a while Mario; remember I'm fixing Ben's boat starting next Saturday. Must go, hope you catch some big ones Mario."

"That's what they say – 'look, hasn't Mario got a big one!" he emulated a high pitched woman's voice, stretching his hands out as if he was telling a fishing story.

Cassie flushed slightly, passing a glance at Mario as she lowered her eyes, not wanting to show embarrassment.

"You know what they say Mario, big feet – small.... Er-hem... I have to go. Have a great weekend. Bye!" she was away before Mario could think of a reply.

Mario watched as Cassie jogged jauntily back to the dock. He kissed the tips of his fingers and waved the kiss toward Cassie's general direction. *Bambina – you will be mine. Soon my little Cassie – soon.*

The troop carrier bounced along a sandy coastal track for about an hour before Karen stopped by a lagoon under the shady umbrella of a gum tree. Karen had kept up a light-hearted conversation, searching for topics Ben might be interested in. She sensed he was distracted. She hoped it wasn't Cassie. *Anyway, I've got him now, he's all mine today.*

"Come on slow coach," Karen beckoned to Ben. "The girls are just going to walk around the lagoon to see if there are any recent bahrru tracks."

"Bahrru?" Ben enquired, suddenly animated.

"Yeah – sorry, crocodile. The salties sometimes come in here, even if it's a fresh water lagoon. Wouldn't want you to get eaten now would we? That'd be a bit of a waste!"

"I could get a knife and pretend I'm Crocodile Dundee?" Ben laughed, but secretly was quite concerned. He had not seen any crocodiles yet. A miner had been killed by a crocodile near an adjoining community. He had been snorkelling at a beach.

"You'll need more than a knife if the local croc's in here – he's a monster!"

It was Mary Djalanga, the senior woman today, who showed Ben how to gather and cut the reeds and grasses they used for weaving their baskets and mats. The Yolngu women laughed bashfully at Ben when he tried to carry too much back to the car and tripped on a fallen branch. He fell face first on the muddy bank; stood up grinning and brushed the mud off his shirt. Karen, seeing the mud on his nose and forehead, quickly scooped up some mud in her fingers and painted streaks on each cheek before Ben had a chance to react.

"Yolngu warrior?" Karen looked around for approval from the Yolngu women. They all laughed, but it was Emily who spoke.

"No – he balanda warrior. White face – black paint!"

"Think you'll find my face is quite red under all this dirt," laughed Ben as he crouched by the water's edge and splashed his face. Karen knelt beside him and dampened a head scarf she had been wearing. She carefully washed Ben's face, her arms raised, breasts squeezed together in a skimpy lime green halter neck top. Ben breathed deeply trying hard not to react like a man; trying hard to suppress his desire, but only breathing in the perfume and scent of a woman – a beautiful woman who wanted him.

The Yolngu women had walked away, not sure what might happen next. Sex was a most natural part of Yolngu lives – men would sometimes just take a woman if she was there for the taking. It was easy to see that Karen was there for the taking. Rose had also told them how balanda Ben, was kissing Cassie when she walked into the art centre. So they knew balanda, or white man was the same as Yolngu man. They pulled back to give Karen some space for sex with this beautiful balanda man.

"Oops – gotta go Karen – call of nature," muttered Ben as he tried to hide the front of his shorts and rushed off into the thicket. *That was close – two beautiful women in one morning. I'm not made of stone – how much longer can I keep fighting this?* He kept looking over his shoulder while pretending to urinate, but Karen hadn't followed – at least she had some class.

Ben returned to the car hoping they might move on; hoping they already had a full load. The women were sorting and placing the bundles of grasses and bark into the back of the troopy, while Karen was just arriving from the lagoon where he had left her. She smiled knowingly, like a cat purring with cream on its whiskers. She had seen Ben's reaction. She knew he wanted her. *It's only a matter of time*, she thought.

It was only a ten minute drive until they emerged at a pristine beach. The white sand stretched about a kilometre in a crescent shape with low scrub covered cliffs at either end. Tiny waves lapped on the shore. The Arafura Sea was docile and stunningly blue this time of year. Karen drove to a sprawling Casuarina tree in the middle of the beach. Rocks and large boulders studded the water, creating a sheltered pool in this isolated spot. No people to be seen. This vast ancient land was unspoiled, unchanged for thousands of years – home and playground to the Yolngu. Ben waited quietly in the shade as the women busied themselves. They were to make a Yolngu barbeque. Some of the women gathered firewood from the shore and nearby bush. They did not have to walk far. Mary dug a large hole in the sand with her hands, while Karen laid out two old grey army blankets punctured with moth holes and mottled dry stains. A stewing pot was filled with sea water and suspended over a fire that was quickly lit. Sarah unwrapped some chunks of kangaroo meat, including two hind legs. The fur was still attached. Two of the other women mixed flour and water kneaded it on a wooden plank, chatting happily in Yolngu language. When much of the wood had turned into hot coals, they were scraped carefully into the hole, the dough wrapped in foil and placed amongst the coals, then covered with sand. Another pot appeared and placed on the fire. Tea was added. Emily smiled at Ben and enquired, "You been Yolngu barbeque before Ben?"

"No – never – it's not like any barbi I've been to before." Ben was thinking how nice it would have been if Cassie could have seen this. This couldn't have been more different from San Francisco.

Karen sensing Ben's distraction, interjected, grabbed hold of his hand and tugged him toward one of the blankets, "Come on Ben. Have a seat, the boiled kangaroo and damper will be ready soon."

Ben sat down on the blanket and removed his shoes and socks. He deliberately threw them a suitable distance away, letting the sun diffuse the tropical sweat and smells. Arms tight around his knees, he gazed out to sea longingly. It's going to be a b*eautiful night for a sail. Hope Cassie fixes my boat soon and properly*. Ben flinched at the memory. Karen stood casually in front of him, removing her sarong, exposing a pale blue bikini bottom, apparently oblivious to the attention she was attracting. It was high cut making her long brown legs seem even longer. Ben could not help but notice. She left her halter-neck top on before sitting right next to Ben, deliberately nestling her calf against his thigh, then more *subtle* leg rubbing as she slid her bottom forward along the blanket. Ben fought his arousal – *brick wall, brick wall*. A technique he had used years ago in public when he had been courting the woman who was later to become his wife. He had become an expert in visualisation techniques when studying sports psychology. Now was a good time to think of brick walls and cool oceans. Now was the time to stay focussed.

"So what's up big boy? You left the planet or somethin'?"

"I was just thinking about a brick wall I once built. Don't know why really."

"You never talk about your past. I know ya came from Sydney, you're a builder and used to be married?" Karen raised her eyebrows, stared at Ben expecting an answer.

"That's right, I was married and now I'm a builder at Umbakala."

"What was she like?" Karen asked softly, eager to break through the veneer, the barrier, the something that made Ben into the strong silent type. She had always been able to have any man she wanted with overt sexual overtures, but Ben was different. He seemed to be able to resist everything she threw at him. Karen was open to a challenge. She would learn new tricks with Ben; she would find out what made him tick and then she would use her main weapon – her brief new bikini.

"She was lovely – but I don't want to talk about it."

"Did she run off with another bloke like Mario's wife?"

"Karen, I said I don't want to talk about it – okay?"

"Sure Ben. I've never been married you know?"

"Uh - huh."

"Yeah – never met the right bloke really. I thought Gary might have been the one, but he was a dag really. Anyway he just ran off when ...," she stopped, her eyes welling up. Ben looked across and immediately saw Karen's pain.

"When – what?" he asked tenderly.

"N-nothin' really, nothin' I couldn't take care of meself. Anyway, Gary started screwin' around with one of the young girls in Dumatja's clan. Gave her grog for sex. What an idiot. He just had no idea – no idea."

"I heard that Cassie was threatened by Dumatja?" Karen seemed relieved that Ben had diverted the subject.

"Yeah – she'd better be careful. Don't know that Mario's going to protect her."

"Mario? He's a pretty strong bloke."

"Yeah, but I reckon he'll go to water at the first sign of trouble. Lucky he doesn't like dark girls. Only goes for the whiteys," she said disdainfully, giving herself away.

"I don't think Dumatja will do anything to Cassie. He's a clan leader – they've got an honour code. I should know, I've learnt a lot from Alanja, Bulangi and the other old men."

"Don't bet on it Ben – don't bet on it." Karen had become serious as she too stared out to the horizon, forgetting for a moment why she was there; why she had invited Ben out for the day. Her own brick walls were being built in her mind, a barrier to her past.

"Tucker ready Karen," announced Emily as she lifted the lid off the stewed kangaroo and ladled out the hairy chunks of meat onto a large battered metal tray. The women gathered round the fires and extracted the foil covered damper. There was a pleasant smell of burnt eucalypt, cooked meat and fresh bread drifting around the camp. Karen expertly ripped the skin off a large chunk of meat while waving away a few flies that had started hovering. She handed Ben a steaming plate of meat and damper, gathered her own food before sitting back down next to Ben again. The women all sat on the other blanket trying politely to chat in English and involve Ben and Karen. It was small talk. Talk about the meat and whose man was the best hunter and how the missionaries had introduced white flour and shown them how to make damper. Ben found the meat gamey and tough, but the blandness of the meal was overtaken by the nature of the occasion. He was sitting on a wild isolated part of the country hardly anyone knew about, let alone had the chance to experience a picnic barbeque, Yolngu style. Yet again, he found himself wishing Cassie had been here to see this. After the women tidied up the first course, they poured strong black tea into enamel mugs and handed them round, while Karen shared out the rest of the damper on paper plates. A large jar of strawberry jam was passed around with a communal knife stuck in the jar for spreading. Dessert.

The sun was still fairly high after they had tidied and washed some of the dishes in one of the rock pools. Ben was pleased they were having a group chat, mostly about Yolngu life styles and history. He was afraid Karen might start prying into his past again. *No one need know.* The past was his business.

Sometime during the afternoon, Ben had stretched out on the edge of the blanket, hat over his eyes, just listening and enjoying the warm sea breeze flowing over his bare legs. He was shocked by a sudden splash of water on his chest and face. Immediately sitting up, blowing salt water out of his mouth, he saw Karen above him in the sunlight – tall brown and almost naked in the briefest of bikinis. She was dripping wet; hips tilted seductively, a football under one arm and a cup in the other hand. An empty cup.

"I came prepared." She grinned, staring into Ben's eyes. Ben's first instinct was to tackle Karen and playfully tickle her while she squirmed in the sand. Laura had thrown water on him once, while he had been napping on a beach. He had chased her, tackled her, kissed her – then ... the memory came back stronger than ever. Laura had been more petite than Karen. She had short blonde hair and was trim and athletic. It had been difficult to catch her on the sand, but then they played – played like only a man and a woman in love could play. In the sand, on an isolated beach near Port Macquarie. He drifted back. The beautiful memory had only taken a second but he knew it would last a lifetime. A life sentence of memories. *I can't do this again. I don't want the complications of a woman.*

"Come on big boy. Remember? We were gonna have a footy game?"

"Yeah – right. Come on girls!" Ben stood up, signalling for the Yolngu women to rise up. They smiled bashfully, but Ben was insistent, pretending to drag them physically but never touching them. Karen's face would have soured cream. This was not her plan. She was sure a game of tackle with Ben would have lead to something – would have made him give in to his desires.

Ben took charge, organising two goal posts with pieces of driftwood, and picking two teams. He made sure Karen was on his side to minimise contact. They played touch football. The women knew the rules already. Touch Football and Australian Rules Football were very popular in Arnhem Land. They had watched their brothers and sons play in the village. Now, they delighted in the game themselves. To them it was like a brief moment of Yolngu women's liberation in an essentially patriarchal society.

The game lasted about half an hour in the hot sun. Sweat glistened on black and white skin, old and young together, as they ran, darted and giggled with each touch. Karen scored two tries and showed displeasure when Ben allowed their opponents to score twice, followed by his sportsman like approval as they celebrated. Suddenly Sarah stopped mid play; pointing out to sea. She uttered only one word and everyone stood still.

"Bahrru!"

The saltwater crocodile appeared like a log with some of his back visible, eyes and tip of his nose protruding above the water. His means of propulsion were hidden as he drifted past the rocks. He was about fifty metres off shore.

"He big one. He live this beach, down other end in creek. That special place for secret men business – we not go there." Emily pointed to the far end of the beach. There was a row of mangroves running along a sand spit and a pile of tall granite boulders in from the shore. Ben looked across the length of the beach and tried to memorise the place in case he ever came here bushwalking.

"I *was* going in for a swim – not now!" Karen did not disguise the disappointment in her voice.

"Yo Karen. You go swim now."

"*Now?* No way! There's a croc out there!"

"No worry Karen when you *see* him. You worry when you *no* see him." Emily was smiling as she moved toward the water. It was higher tide now, but the rocks still appeared to offer protection from the bahrru. They all stood quietly watching as he drifted further along the beach. Satisfied he wasn't staying, the Yolngu women all waded into the water with their clothes still on, settling in the shallows, but still facing in the direction of the crocodile.

"I'm game if you are," said Ben to no one in particular as he ripped off his shirt, exposing his strong tanned pectorals and sprinted toward the water, entering with a shallow belly flop for maximum splash. The women all laughed and splashed him back. Karen gingerly followed, walking in slowly as if the water was cold. She was the only one who didn't laugh or smile and it wasn't long before she returned to the safety of the blanket on the shore.

As they headed for home Ben chatted to the Yolngu women while Karen drove. Karen had been unusually quiet for the whole trip. Ever since they had gone into the water, Ben had seemed determined to ask all these questions about Yolngu culture. She had not been able to say much or change the subject. Today had not gone as she had planned. *Oh well, there's still tonight. It's Saturday night – party time for Ben!*

Like most men, Ben usually missed the signals; the signals that women sent to men when they were interested. The extra flash of breasts, the extra long eye contact, the innocent touches on the arm. With Karen, Ben was left in no doubt. He knew she wanted him. She was beautiful – it had not been easy resisting. He had not had sex for a long time – sex with Laura – the first time had been like the moon falling out of the sky, planets spinning around inside his head, explosions like asteroids sending him out into an orbit of love and pleasure, like he had never imagined possible – couldn't imagine having again. Laura was not like Karen. She was a virgin when they had married. She said she had waited just for him. She was gone. *My beautiful Laura – gone for good. Without Laura there was no hope.* He had to get away from Karen – at least for tonight. He needed time to think about Cassie and Karen and all these unwanted desires. *Time away from people.*

As they finally approached the village, everyone was silent. Weariness had settled on them all after the end of a busy day.

"Karen, do you mind dropping me off at the dock first? I'm keen to do a few important jobs before getting an early night."

"Oh. I thought. I thought you and I might have a little party tonight Ben. I wanted to say thank you for your help collecting the bark today. I've got some frozen pizza and wine." She asked hopefully, but had already resigned herself to another night alone. *She* had read Ben's signals – loud and clear.

It was not hard for Cassie to read the signals either, as she watched Karen spin the wheels of the troopy, fishtailing slightly as she accelerated. Ben was walking along the dock without looking back. Karen raised a cloud of dust behind her as the car disappeared from sight. *Hmm, Karen's not going to be in a great mood on Monday.* The work on her boat was done and Cassie was relaxing to the soothing music of Norah Jones, as she sat in the cockpit thinking about how to prepare her dinner. Just as Ben came level with Serendipity, the next track came on *'come away with me ...in the night ...'*

"I don't think so Cassie, not without a rudder – and the way you steer with sails ..."

Cassie's pleasant mood dissolved at his hurtful comment. *Why couldn't Ben just forget? Why did he have to keep rubbing it in? It was after all an accident.*

"You going to keep playing that broken record all year Ben Brogan? There's only so many times I can say sorry!"

Ben grinned at Cassie. A cheeky grin – his eyes mischievous. Pleased he had managed to set the agenda for the evening, he was sure now Cassie would be kept at a distance. He did not respond right away. He looked up and down the shiny decks and polished winches. He saw the neatly stored sails; the tide bundles of ropes – the mark of a good sailor.

"I see you've been busy. She looks good. What's her cruising speed?" Ben just could not resist talking about sailing.

Cassie was taken aback by this sudden change of demeanour and change of subject. She loved Serendipity. They had been through so much together. There was that storm soon after she had sailed from the Cook Islands. The only problem she had on the journey was that rudder. Shame it had set them off to such a bad start.

She started telling Ben about her boat and some of the trip across the Pacific. The re-living was so real that she almost forgot Ben's presence. Cassie suddenly stopped her monologue and looked at Ben squatting on the dock. His eyes were soft and glazed over; she become conscious that Ben had been looking into her eyes unblinking, the whole time, hand clasping his chin like a law professor considering a weighty brief.

"Sorry Ben, I've been talking too much. I didn't mean to bore you ..."

"I'm not bored – far from it." Ben spoke softly and slowly.

"Listen, while I was working, I prised off a couple of those molluscs off the dock and used them for bait. Caught a little shark – cleaned it, but there's too much for me. Would you like some barbequed shark?" Before Ben could reply, she added quickly, "But, I want to get an early night ..."

"That sounds fine Cassie. Two barbi's in one day. Must be my lucky day. Now I'll only come if you let me bring the wine and salad. I've got a new bottle of Pinot Grigio in the fridge. It's too good to drink on my own"

Cassie's eyes sparkled. *It's my favourite wine too.* She gulped as Ben stood up, stretching his arms behind his head, exposing strong tanned biceps.

"My favourite! Deal! I'll just light the gas barbi on the back of my boat and cook the fish, if you go and make the salad?" Ben noticed that she had raised her tone at the end of the sentence, just like an Aussie. She was starting to remind him of another Aussie he once knew – intimately. Ben kicked himself for asking about Serendipity. He reminded himself, *It's just dinner, then an early night – I mustn't get too close.*

Cassie had set up a folding table that attached to the compass stand in the cockpit and set the table with cutlery, plates and plastic mugs when Ben arrived with the salad and wine. Minutes later the shark steaks were cooked. She had fried them with olive oil, garlic and a heavy dousing of lemon, just the way he liked them. The sun was a large red ball above the horizon and the boat was rocking ever so gently with the remains of the day's sea breeze.

"To growling lions and little Goldilocks." Cassie raised her plastic mug in a mock toast when they were half way through dinner. They had each eaten quietly, not talking, like two sparring partners not wanting to make the first move – sizing each other up. Ben thought about responding with the 'big bad girl wolves and innocent little piggies', but held back. He was still not happy with the damage to his new boat, yet here he was, being softened up by the person, the woman who had smashed his boat.

They clinked mugs and sipped on the cool ambrosia. Cassie noted Ben's lack of response. *Just as well – I don't want to get too close to this man. He's only here because I had too much fish and he's keen to listen to my sailing tales.*

"So how was your day with all those women? Karen show you a good time?" Cassie bit her tongue when she realised the innuendo. She hadn't meant it. It had just come out wrong.

"We had a wow of a time. We had a Yolngu barbi on the beach, then a game of footy before we swam with the crocs."

"Was that smart?"

"We had to do it. After all, Karen had brought her bikini – couldn't let that go to waste. Didn't leave much to the imagination either." Ben forced a smile, but it looked convincing enough to Cassie.

"Well I'm sure you got more than an eye full." Cassie's mouth curled to one side, trying to appear cheerful, trying to recapture the mood they had shared that morning. Ben did not answer; he stared over Cassie's shoulder at the last splash of orange in the sky. The sun had already gone down and Cassie decided to change the subject.

"So have you given any thought to the repair work needed at the art centre yet?" Ben stared at Cassie. He crossed his arms and rose to his feet.

"Thanks for the dinner Cassie. I have to go." He grabbed the empty salad bowl, rose to his feet, then sprung nimbly onto the dock, barely rocking the boat, before turning back briefly, "By the way, that was one of my favourite songs."

Cassie watched him leave, anger and sadness rising in her throat. She breathed deeply to chase away the tears. Bitter regret overwhelmed her at her rude comment. *But still, he's made these suggestions about Mario and me. Just like a man. Not willing to take as much as he gives. Run away – don't talk about it – just run away.*

7   Yolngu Church

Sunday morning and Cassie had slept in. She lay dozily in her snug v-berth, relishing the morning breeze tumbling over her body through the open hatch – a cooling caress. Newspapers and croissants. The memory of past Sundays in San Francisco – waking up in her apartment, listening to the sea gulls squawking in the bay, the doorbell ringing, James arriving with the hot croissants. Cassie would make the coffee and on warm days they would breakfast on the balcony and read the Sunday papers. That part was good, but she always became restless – wanted to do more – go sailing, hiking, surfing – anything, just to get out and experience living. James would have happily sat on her balcony all day drinking coffee. Cassie lingered at the thought of James. *I wonder how he's doing. I hope he's found someone – a female couch potato.* She laughed at this new picture. A picture of James and his chubby new girlfriend sitting on the couch, eating crisps and watching TV.

Cassie slid out of bed, feet meeting the cool fibreglass floor. Slipping off her light cotton pyjamas, she opened the door of the only wardrobe, which had a mirror attached to the inside. Turning slowly, Cassie scrutinised her figure – tanned legs rising up to meet her pale bottom, which she squeezed, face wrinkling with distaste. *Hmmm, dimples – cellulite on my butt – still, not too much yet. Maybe one day I'll find Mr Right and, have his babies before he notices? Need to make sure he only ever sees me from the front.* Cassie chuckled to herself as she brushed her hair, her firm breasts bobbing pertly with each stroke. Suddenly she jumped. Heavy footsteps on the dock. Clutching at her nakedness, Cassie jumped back under the sheet, but not before seeing a pair of familiar strong legs through the porthole. Ben! He kept walking. She slowly emerged from the berth and crept toward the hatch. Could he have seen her from there? She heard a car drive up. Wrapped in the sheet, Cassie peered outside, to watch Ben climbing into a troopy driven by Garrawarra.

Ben had woken with the sun. He usually did. It had been a restless, frustrating night. His hormones were over-flowing and disturbingly close to him on the next boat was a gorgeous petite woman. Again and again he re-wound little videos in his mind of Cassie in her brief, work shorts, bending over to scoop fish off her barbeque. He had watched her crossing and uncrossing her legs; her curves more elegant than the finest cruising yacht. She had stretched and wiggled her toes as she talked about her journey – her hands and fingers talked to him like ghostly Polynesian dancers revealing their mystery of erotic sensuality. Then, his movie changed to Karen in her flimsy bikini, cavorting on the beach; dusky, burning sexuality...

A mug of strong coffee, some bread and cheese was all Ben needed to start the day, as he sat in his cockpit daydreaming. He kept looking across to Serendipity – no sign of Cassie stirring. As soon as he heard Garrawarra's arrival, he bounded on to the dock and walked towards the troopy, relieved that Cassie was still asleep and he did not have to face her after last night. Mischievously though, he made his step noisier beside Serendipity as he glanced down through the first porthole. His eyes popped. *Wow! What a figure – what a bum!* He didn't falter – did not miss a step – heart racing, he convinced himself not to look back. Yes, she was beautiful, but she had fallen for Mario's charms – no women for him. *Not now – maybe never.*

Rose had invited Cassie to go with her to church and Cassie had agreed, even though she wasn't a regular church goer. She was a little worried; what should she wear to a Yolngu church? How would the Yolngu receive her? Deep in a plastic storage box were the last of her fresh clothes. Cassie took out a loose fitting blue skirt with a dolphin pattern and a plain white cotton blouse that hung loosely at her waist, hiding her trim figure. Her new sandals were aging prematurely and already impregnated with orange dust that she couldn't scrub off. She had just enough time to make it to the ten o'clock service.

The church was a tall building showing its age; wooden boards with strips of peeling faded paint and side walls almost entirely of small glass louvers. Most of the louvers were open to allow any breezes through; many of them broken and those that weren't, were covered in dust. The church was on a familiar road – just before the council office and surrounded by sand that had been placed around the building and under the nearby gum trees. Clean seating for Yolngu ceremonies and meetings.

As Cassie rushed along the road toward the church, a Yolngu family was walking up to the entrance. They were all clean and fresh like a collective rainbow – the children laughed whilst the three of them competed to hold their father's hand. A number of dusty cars were parked nearby – none of them locked and those that still had windows, were open.

Cassie stopped for a moment when she heard a guitar, electric keyboard and drums, the sound overlaid with the most beautiful women's voices singing Yolngu hymn in harmony. Continuing on to the entrance, Rose's face was there, lit up as their eyes met.

"Miss Cassie – glad you come. Come inside – come in."

Cassie had never seen Rose this animated. Inside was surprisingly clean. There were plain wooden pews, far from full and only Yolngu to be seen – people she hadn't met before except for two of the artists, Emily and Sarah who were out in front singing. Scanning the room, her eyes moved to one white man sitting near the front of the church with an aboriginal family. It was Ben. Cassie tried not to, but continued staring at the back of his head as Rose led her past the worshippers to one of the middle pews where her husband Bulangi and family were seated. Just then, Ben looked around at their rustling– straight at Cassie. Cassie instantly looked down, hoping he had not seen her staring. Her cheeks suddenly felt warm. Had Ben seen her naked this morning?

Cassie settled down next to Rose just as one of the elders stood up at the front and greeted everyone in both Yolngu and English. It was Alanja, council president; the man who had let her into the council building when she had first arrived. Cassie noted how different he looked. He was wearing neat black trousers and a white short sleeved shirt with a collar. Rose whispered in Cassie's ear, that the short man with the white shirt sitting in the front row was the Fijian minister. Cassie already knew that there had been some Fijians who came as missionaries in the fifties. Some had stayed. The Fijians had also introduced kava into the community, a mind numbing drink that was used in traditional Fijian ceremony. It had now become the drug of choice for many Yolngu in Arnhem Land.

The announcements over, the congregation stood and started singing the most mournful hymn. Cassie glanced around. There were only about fifty people, but the heart-felt passion of this angelic choir made Cassie choke up. Tears came to her eyes; Rose sensing Cassie's emotion took her hand and gently, knowingly squeezed. Cassie could not understand these feelings. The Presbyterian hymns in San Leandro had not done this to her. The choir there had worn matching blue robes and the church was immaculate – it could not have been more different. More surprises. Ben was singing. He was holding a sheet of paper. *They must be Yolngu words to the hymns,* thought Cassie as she stood silently; trying hard to maintain her composure.

The Fijian minister preached in English on love and forgiveness. Cassie felt as if he was talking directly to her and she was led to think about Dumatja. Love her enemy? How could she find it in her heart to love and forgive Dumatja? It was hard enough with Ben. And she wondered about Ben, would he forgive her for the damage she'd caused to his boat. They caught each other's eyes across the church before Cassie looked away, seeing a Yolngu woman with a plaster cast on her arm and a swollen eye; so swollen, she could barely see out of it. She looked sad. *I wonder if that's Dumatja's wife?*

By the time the service had finished, Cassie had composed herself and was being introduced to Rose's extended family. Emily and Sarah came across and they all began to chat excitedly about their plans for the rest of the day. Cassie was feeling encouraged again at the welcome she had been shown from the women artists, when she felt a tap on her shoulder. As she swung around, the women went quiet, their eyes on Ben.

"I didn't expect to see *you* here?"

"Why not? Do you think you have exclusive rights on piety?" said Cassie, immediately biting her lip. Regret.

"Me? Sorry, I'm far from pious. I think you of all people should know that. I just wanted to say hi.... Anyway – see you later, I'm having lunch with Garrawarra." Ben turned and walked away. There were no smiles exchanged today. *Why does he bring out the worst in me? Why do I take the bait?*

Cassie woke up well after dawn, back in her house again and ready to face the new week. This time she had locked the front doors and checked the locks twice before going to bed. Rose had invited her to lunch with her family after the church service, then she had walked for most of the afternoon, exploring the bay and a number of nearby beaches. Low tide below some rocky cliffs had revealed the most stunning coloured rocks, corals and tiny sea creatures, quite unlike anything she had seen on the Californian coastline. A man and woman with their three children had been gathering shells off the rocks, presumably for their dinner. Cassie wished *she* was a little girl again, holding her dad's hand as they had crab-finding competitions and searched for shells with the most interesting patterns.

After completing some simple administration tasks, Cassie agreed with Karen about her goals for the day. As she had suspected, Karen was cool and unfriendly. Her arms stayed folded for the whole of their meeting and her responses to Cassie's attempts at conversation were brief. Cassie remembered her speeding off in the car on Saturday and knew better than to ask about the trip to the bush with Ben and the artists. *I guess she'll talk about it if she wants to.*

"Karen, I'm going to see Mike and hopefully spend most of the day with the book-keeper. I need to find out why we're losing money. Will you be okay?"

"Yeah. No worries, plenty here to do." Karen was subdued, but Cassie was confident she would do the agreed tasks well. Karen was a good worker.

Again, Cassie was able to walk into the council building with no one approaching her – no one in the office asking if they could help. She popped her head round the door of Mike's office just as the phone rang. Cassie looked around to see if anyone would come to answer it, then decided to do it herself.

"Hello, Mike Britliff's phone – Cassie speaking."

"Oh, g'day, this is Cummings hardware in Darwin. Look, there's an order here for building supplies for a Darwin job. We need to know Mr Britliff's address to send the invoice."

Cassie paused for a second, before taking the initiative,

"I expect you'll mark it to Mr Britliff's attention here at Umbakala Council – or, better still, here's a fax machine, I'll just give you the number." A few minutes later, Cassie picked up the fax from the machine. She examined it, and then looked again. It did not seem to make sense. Tucking the invoice into her folder, she walked down the corridor to the book-keeper's office. They had met briefly last week.

"Hi Lesley, I was looking for Mike. Is he still in Darwin?"

"He's always in Darwin. I reckon he spends more time in Darwin than Umbakala! Come in, grab yourself a chair Cassie." Lesley was a small woman, Cassie guessed in her mid-forties. She had short peroxide hair, the brightest red lipstick and thick layered make up. The tell-tale line began at one ear, crossed her neck and finished under the other ear. She wore a mini skirt; stockings and a tight satin blouse which exposed a long cleavage line making her breasts look like they were glued together. Cassie wondered why anyone would want to wear stockings in this heat.

"Lesley, Mike told me that the art centre is in financial difficulties and I don't really understand why? I've looked at our sales figures and they look quite good. Do you have any ideas?"

"Look luvvy, I just add them up, I don't analyse them. I leave that stuff to Mike. I can give you the reports for the last couple of years though if you like?"

"That would be great Lesley. Could I have a look at the payments and invoices as well please?"

"No worries Cassie. You can use the empty office next door." Lesley stood up, pulled a mountain of files off her shelves and carried them in three loads to the office next door.

"Just give me a yell if you need help with anything." She smiled broadly; lipstick stains on her teeth.

Cassie started checking the records, but couldn't help wondering about Lesley. What was she hiding from? What had brought her to this far flung hiding place? She looked more like a barmaid than a book-keeper. Still, somehow she made Cassie feel prudish as she compared her own modest skirt and top which hid her figure. Cassie banished her thoughts as she started digging into the files. Her mom had given her a good grounding in book-keeping and a basic knowledge in accounting, which enabled her to interpret the profit and loss reports and ledger accounts and work out exactly what was happening with the finances of the art centre but it was time-consuming. She worked methodically for hours, stopping only to accept Lesley's offer of a sandwich and cup of coffee. She summarised data, copied payments and receipts vouchers as she organised her findings into two files, one for the art centre and one for the housing project. A nagging suspicion aroused by that phone call, demanded a deeper forensic audit than she had planned. Cassie hated the feeling that she was being distrustful but her integrity meant that she just could not let this go. Cassie had perhaps learnt or inherited from her parents, a philosophy on trust. She always preferred to trust people, to take them at face value and allow herself to be disappointed if they betrayed that trust. Now, here she was, acutely suspicious that Mike was both incompetent and dishonest. *But what can I do? Who do I show my findings? Who can I trust with this information? Can somebody do something about this, or will it just get buried under the carpet like it has been?*

At four o'clock, Cassie rang Karen at the Art centre.

"Karen, sorry I've been gone for so long. I've found some interesting stuff in the books. Could you do me a favour and lock up please? I still need to finish up here."

"No worries Cassie. It's been a quiet day and I've been able to tidy up the stock in the store room. A couple of new works arrived – that's about it really."

"Okay, see you in the morning – we'll talk more then." Cassie hung up and wondered if there was any point in sharing much of her findings with Karen. She was good with the art displays and sales, but had little understanding of finances. *Who can I talk to about this?* The thought lingered and troubled her as she gathered the files and prepared to leave the office.

The last of the day's sea breeze rippled through the gum leaves beside the road as Cassie walked down toward her house. Looking across, she saw the concrete block foundations of the house the Yolngu men were building under Ben's direction. There was no one there. Cassie looked at her watch, surprised to see how late it was. The sun was slipping fast beyond the horizon. Startled by the clang of a steel door shutting, Cassie looked to the builder's compound and shed. There was Ben with Garrawarra, locking up the tools for the night. Her heart raced. She tried to remain calm. Maybe she could talk to Ben? He already had some sort of conflict with Mike – maybe she should share her findings? *But then maybe he'll get angry again or claim he's too busy to help, like with the art centre repairs? Maybe he'll bring up his damaged boat again?* Forgetting her pride, Cassie took a deep breath and walked toward the men. They had seen her by now, but continued chatting and laughing together.

Ben was the first to see Cassie walking toward them. She was smiling. *Such a happy smile,* thought Ben as he realised how often he had seen her smiling with other people; with Karen, Mike, Rose, the women at church, Mario – yes- Mario. *Just not that often with me,* he guessed.

"Hi Ben. Sorry to interrupt, Garrawarra."

"That okay Cassie," said Garrawarra his huge set of perfect white teeth flashing, "I rushing home – wife cooking turtle. Cousin catch today."

"Turtle? What does that taste like?" Cassie was still smiling.

"Ben reckon taste like chicken!" Garrawarra's replied as he pushed Ben off balance, as only a friend could.

"Yeah and dugong tastes like pork, but I'm never eating that green slimy turtle fat again!" Ben gently punched Garrawarra's arm, "Cassie, did you know that slimy green turtle fat is a Yolngu delicacy?"

"Ooh – yum – better than McDonald's hamburger," said Garrawarra, rubbing circles round his belly.

"Hey, I come from the land of hamburger, don't knock it!" laughed Cassie, joining in the repartee.

"Gotta go. You want come eat turtle tonight Cassie? Always room for one more."

"Next time thanks Garrawarra. There's something I need to talk to Ben about – about work."

There was a long pause as they watched Garrawarra stride off jauntily. *He seems so happy,* thought Cassie. He had a wife, an armful of children, turtle for dinner but not much else. Cassie had thought often about happiness in recent months. She had seen so much happiness among the native islanders at Penrhyn and Fiji. She noticed that often those that had less were more willing to give, to share what they had with others. Here was Garrawarra, working to feed a large family, hardly any income, yet willing to share his food, his delicacies with her. Sometimes she just felt overawed by their generosity.

"What do you want to see me about Cassie?" Ben's voice was quiet and gentle. She had heard this tone before during some of the good moments they had shared. She hoped it would stay this way after she told him what he had found.

"I don't know where to start Ben. I spent nearly all day looking through accounting records at council. I think I found some – how can I put this – improprieties?"

"What, with the art centre finances?"

"Yep, that and maybe the housing fund as well."

"Really? I'd be very interested in having a look Cassie. I don't trust that bastard Mike as far as I could throw him"

Cassie grinned at the image before responding,

"I was just on my way home to put together some sort of report from these documents. Would you like to come round to dinner and I'll show you what I've got?" Cassie almost bit off the end of that sentence. She was getting used to Mario picking up on the slightest double entendre.

"That would be great Cassie. To tell you the truth, I'm getting a little tired of my one-pot wonders. What's on the menu?"

Cassie duly noted Ben's lack of an inappropriate reply. She could not help but compare the two men and remembered how she and her colleagues in the art staff room would give marks out of ten for any new male teacher who would arrive at the school. *Ben would get a 9 for legs, 9.5 for body, 7 for handsome*, thought Cassie. *Hmm, Mario gets an 8.5 for handsome, 7 for humour, but 3 for some of his behaviour.* Putting these thoughts behind her, Cassie began to tell Ben about the process of the day's audit. He listened quietly as they began to feel more comfortable in each other's company again, yet there was a tension, a kind of electric charge that somehow remained between them, just waiting for someone to flick a switch.

They were soon in Cassie's kitchen, Ben slicing carrots and peeling potatoes, while Cassie made a sauce for the chicken which was slowly pan frying. They talked about sailing. Cassie wanted to hear about Ben's voyage north from Sydney and through the famous Whitsunday Islands. Ben in turn listened attentively at Cassie's story of her Pacific voyage. Before long, they sat down to eat. As he listened to Cassie, Ben remembered Laura and how they talked about sailing and dolphins and desert islands. He loved that there were moments she could talk like a bloke about mainsails and jib sheets, yet all the time, she was a real woman. He had never met any woman like Laura since. Until now – but he was still wary. He had been on his own now for two years and getting used to single life – single celibate life. As they sat finishing the last few mouthfuls of their meal Cassie changed the mood with a question.

"So why did you leave Sydney to come to this isolated place? People up here seem to be running away from something."

"Maybe I'm running *towards* something rather than running away. What about you Cassie, what are you running away from?"

Before Cassie could answer, they both turned their heads toward the front door. The house shook slightly as heavy footsteps could be heard bounding up the stairs. A knot quickly re-appeared in Cassie's stomach as she remembered Dumatja's sudden appearance last week. There was a loud knock at the door as Ben looked at Cassie and saw the fear on her face.

"Want me to get that?" Without waiting for a reply, he rose to his feet and walked calmly to the door.

"G'day Ben. What are *you* doin' here mate?"

"Nothing I shouldn't be doing, mate. Friend here to see you," said Ben looking back at Cassie, his face impassive, before resuming his seat at the dining table.

"Hi Mario. Ben and I have just had dinner. Sorry we haven't any left; can I get you a glass of wine?"

"Hey Cassie, I thought you were my girl? What's goin' on?"

"*Your* girl?" She raised her voice, "Whatever gave you that idea Mario? What? A couple of meals and two nights riding shotgun in case a crazed Yolngu man attacked me again?" Cassie was indignant. *Men and their assumptions!*

"Come off it – it wasn't just riding shotgun you wanted me for, baby," Mario was grinning, hands on hips. He turned slightly and winked at Ben with bravado.

"You rude arrogant ..." She did not finish the sentence; instead, Cassie counted to three under her breath, then spoke slowly, quite deliberately. "I'd like you to leave Mario – now!"

"Em, I just came to tell you. Your resin has arrived." He looked uncertainly at Ben, perhaps looking for some male approval. Ben was staring at Mario, trying hard to size up the situation. He had thought Mario and Cassie had been sleeping together. He knew Mario's reputation with some of the nurses. Now he wasn't so sure. Not that it mattered. What Cassie got up to was her business. He did not want any more women – women just brought pain. *Too much pain,* he thought as he remembered Laura; *Beautiful Laura,* his wife.

"Thank you Mario. I'll pick it up on Saturday morning, okay? Maybe we could start this conversation again on Saturday when you've learnt how to behave!" Cassie held the front door open for Mario as he ambled out grinning. He paused in the doorway and smirked at Cassie, then blew her a kiss as he stepped outside.

"Bella bambina ..."

The mood had been sobered by the interruption. Ben and Cassie finished the last of their meal in silence. While Ben washed up the dishes, Cassie started telling Ben the details of her findings in the books.

"So apart from all those payments to Dumatja, which I can't tie in with his art sales, here are two invoices for $2,000 for repairs to an outboard motor. Robert Datjun's name is on the invoice. Who's he?"

"Datjun? He's one of Dumatja's mob. His wife Emily goes to church. See her with a black eye now and then."

"I saw a woman with a cast on her arm and bruises on her face at church. Who was she?"

"That's George Dumatja's wife. He'll probably kill her one day and there's nothing anyone can do about it."

Cassie shivered at the mention of Dumatja's name, before continuing with her findings.

"Then there are cash takings that have never been banked. That puts Karen, Lesley or Mike in the frame, except Karen wouldn't be so stupid as to write up the sale and then steal the money?"

"I don't think it would be Lesley either. I know she looks a bit rough but I think she's honest. It's that sleaze bag Mike. It's got to be. Anything else out of the ordinary?"

"Yep, your housing fund. I took a call from a building supplies guy in Darwin. He wanted to know Mike's address to send an account to. I asked him to fax it and it showed materials being delivered to a Darwin address."

"That doesn't prove anything; he might be building a private house there; nothing to do with council."

"That's what I thought, but then I checked different supplier's invoices. Look at this," Cassie showed him the copies. "Concrete and steel paid for by council out of the building fund. Look at the delivery address. Same Darwin address."

Ben examined the invoices. He sat quietly absorbing this information. There seemed to be no doubt. Mike was building a house for himself in Darwin and Umbakala Council was paying for it.

"Can I hang onto these Cassie? I think Mike comes back on Thursday. I'm going up there to put a rocket under him. We might have to go to the police or the Northern Territory Government with this. Someone has to stop these thieving bastards."

They sat outside for the rest of the evening rocking gently on the same seat where Mario had made amorous advances. This time Cassie did not feel the need to hug the corner of the seat. The night was warm, but Cassie felt goose bumps all over her body as Ben told her stories of sailing adventures. He made her laugh with the way he teased her with the stories, leaving her hanging in suspense as he went back inside to top up their wine glasses. When he returned he even mentioned Laura.

"What happened to Laura? She was your wife, right?" Cassie asked gently, resting her hand on Ben's arm, before quickly withdrawing it. She did not want to lead him on, it just felt natural. She felt even more comfortable with Ben, but the shivers frightened her. She must keep her distance. *Just friendship that's all; just friendship.*

"Look Cassie; I've never told anyone about Laura. I'm not ready to talk about her just yet. Maybe another time, it's getting late. Will you be okay? I mean with the Dumatja thing?"

"I think so Ben. Thanks for asking. You can stay the night in the spare room if you like?" she raised her eyebrows and smiled. Ben felt weak watching her soft lips curving upwards, her mouth open just slightly. He could see her tongue and teeth and suddenly remembered *that* kiss. That kiss that everyone saw. There was no one looking now, if he kissed her now no one would see. He took a step nearer. He felt himself smiling, saw

Cassie tilt her head, her eyes, dreamy and tired. For an eternity neither one moved but two hearts were racing, when suddenly, they both jumped. An owl's hoot in a nearby tree! No rock music tonight.

"I'd better be going," Ben stood up and reached out both hands. Cassie felt the strength in his arms as he pulled her gently out of the love seat. He leaned forward slowly. Cassie's breath was trapped in her chest as she felt the rough stubble of his cheek brush against hers with the gentlest touch, then his lips softly pecking her cheek.

"Goodnight Cassie." He smiled again and looked longingly in her eyes – still holding her hands. He turned and skipped lightly down the stairs. An athlete's skip. Cassie put a hand to her cheek where the feeling of his kiss lingered as she stared into the blackness – this wild blackness full of poisonous snakes, crocodiles, buffalo and other things that kill. Yolngu witch doctors.

8 The Axe and the Art Centre

For the next two days, Cassie was able to busy herself in the art centre. Karen was still cool with her but did her work well and managed to show friendly enthusiasm whenever a customer arrived. Cassie had time to make some minor adjustments to the art centre web page and spent time inserting a photograph of each artist together with a paragraph describing their background and showing their latest works for sale. This proved lucrative almost immediately with a number of internet sales, from as far away as Japan, France and the US. *At least the internet sales can't be tampered with*, thought Cassie as she entered the sales in their journal. She was able to make further plans for the Garma festival, at times working with Rose. Sweet, gentle Rose. She had finally been able to talk to Cassie about her mother's funeral which was to start on Friday, in the middle of the day. Rose invited Cassie to come and Cassie, who had felt awkward, unsure if she would be welcome, had agreed to close the art centre for the afternoon. She did not know what to expect, but she knew it was a chance to witness ancient ceremonial practices, closed to most white people and she wanted to show her support to Rose. She felt honoured that Rose was now a friend and she had been invited into her family to mourn, to celebrate in the life and death of Yolngu, as they had been doing for thousands of years.

Thursday morning, Ben had spent two hours with the men, showing them how to cut and tie the steel reinforcing for the concrete slab floor. Garrawarra had quickly understood the concepts and had taken over the supervising job. In the days since Cassie had revealed to him the apparent fraud, Ben had been seething inside and planning in his mind the *discussion* with Mike. He was aware how angry he had become in the last two years. He hated himself for his sudden outburst when before he would approach crises calmly and coolly – as a problem-solving exercise – something to be sorted rather than to become emotional over. It would be hard to remain in control when confronting Mike.

Papers in hand, Ben strode into the council offices, a grim expression on his face. He knew Mike was in; the shiny Land Cruiser was parked out the front of the council building. He smiled as he passed the receptionist, her head down, sorting the mail.

"Namirri Djingala."

"Namirri Ben – you here to see Mike?"

"Yo – I'll just go right in."

"Sorry Ben – he say no want see anyone today. Too busy."

"This can't wait Djingala. Don't worry, I'll tell him you tried to stop me." He continued on down the dingy corridor, where he saw Mike's door was closed. He knocked twice before he swung open the door. Mike looked up over his reading glasses; the air conditioner was on, but Mike still had sweat saturating his pale blue shirt. The drops on his pink top lip became rivulets as he blurted, "What the ... I can't see you today, I'm very busy. Make an appointment with Djingala for next week." He did his best to look down, pretending to look at a document avoiding eye contact with Ben. Ben slammed down his papers on the edge of the desk and in a deep voice of steel, he spoke – slowly.

"You'll make time for me – NOW!"

Startled, Mike put his hands against the desk and pushed his chair backwards away from Ben. His eyes widened and more beads of perspiration appeared on his balding head.

"W-what do you want that can't wait?" His voice was higher pitched than usual.

"I want you to tell me about building your house in Darwin and Umbakala Council paying for materials! I want you to tell me about Art Centre cash going missing! I want you to tell me about money from the art centre paying for Robert Datjun's motor boat! I want you to tell me why I shouldn't go to the police with this information!" Ben pointed to the files as he spoke, then crossed his arms and stood like the Colossus of Rhodes – eyes transfixed, unblinking – on Mike. Mike started to bluster; he was used to attack being the best form of defence.

"How dare you? What right have you to come in here and threaten me? I ought to sack you right here on the spot – and that scheming Cassie Greenway too. She's been nothing but trouble since she got here." He watched Ben's eyes widen with surprise. Mike sat up straighter in his chair, sensing an advantage. "That's right! I know she was in here snooping on Monday. Lesley told me."

"Sack me? We've got evidence to send you to gaol mister – this is theft!" Ben prodded his fingers at the papers he had dumped on Mike's desk.

"Listen, you know nothing about how to run a place like this or the way things are done with *these* people. In the first place, I have an *arrangement* with council to buy all building materials from the same suppliers – yours and mine, so we can get a volume discount. Did your snoopy friend find where I made repayments?"

Ben stared blankly on hearing this information. He started to have a slight doubt – maybe they were wrong about Mike? He wondered if Cassie could have missed something?

Mike had been in this type of conflict situation before. He had managed several aboriginal communities before and was no stranger to accusations. He smugly sensed their weaknesses – he sensed Ben's doubt, saw it in his eyes – time to go in for the kill.

"Now look," he spoke more quietly this time, trying to smile, but what Ben saw was a sneer, as a corner of his mouth was raised. "I'm willing to forget all about this outburst and wild accusations. Why don't we make an appointment to talk, say next Friday? We'll invite Charlie Alanja – I believe you're on good terms with our shire president? I'll show you both the building accounts. Show you some real evidence – okay?"

"What about the art centre? The missing cash?"

"We'll have a look at that too. Okay Ben? Now if you don't mind, I've got a lot of work to get through." He settled back to reading his papers, dismissing Ben with the action.

Ben stared for a moment at Mike's balding head, then slowly picked up his bundle of papers.

"Nine o'clock Friday week. I'll bring Cassie." He turned and strode out as purposefully as he had entered, out of the empty office and into the dry heat outside. Ben felt at that moment as if he had let Cassie down. He had confronted Mike with what he thought was irrefutable evidence. Was his gut-feel right? Was Mike the scoundrel he appeared to be? He was still sure, but there was a niggle of doubt deep in his mind. What if they could not find the proof in the paperwork? There were now concerns he might have lost his job and Cassie's. He liked working with the Yolngu men. It was a far cry from his building projects – cottages for well-heeled middle classes. Here he was helping people to help themselves. Giving the Yolngu men a chance to find meaning and purpose in their lives instead of taking 'sit down money' and playing cards and smoking gunja all day. Ben went back to the building site where the men had nearly finished laying the steel mesh. He would talk to Cassie about the meeting on the weekend. Saturday they would work on his boat. He hoped Cassie knew what she was doing with fibreglass – his boat was too important to him to be ruined by poor workmanship. His boat was now his life, his home.

Cassie was in at the art centre early on Friday morning. She had welcomed the quiet evenings to herself, a chance to catch up with her reading; a chance to email her family and friends. She did not tell them everything, not wanting the people back home to worry about her. Cassie had however sent a girly email to her best friend. Rhoda had gone to art school with her and they had been lucky in getting work placements at the same high school. Cassie felt a twinge of jealousy at the news that Rhoda was now three months pregnant. Mostly, Cassie was delighted, as she knew that Rhoda and her husband had been trying to have a baby for two years. She had comforted a teary Rhoda with each of the three miscarriages and they lived through the shared despair of never having children. Now Cassie had that fear alone. She was past thirty. Why hadn't she found someone yet? Mr Right, where was he? She felt that it would not be long before she was forty and it would all be too late – all she would have was her career, whatever that was at the moment. It was Rhoda who had encouraged her to 'go for it' with Mario. Rhoda had encouraged her to stop saving herself and have some fun, just like she and John had done before they got married. Cassie imagined herself married to Mario and living her life in the boatshed with nappies hanging from a line out the back strung between two gum trees. She thought about how Mario really wanted her, how he had rescued her on the day she had arrived in Umbakala. She thought how nice it felt to be wanted. But then there was Ben and that unexpected kiss. She had thought for a moment he would kiss her again the other night, but it was only a peck on the cheek. There was something holding him back; something troubling him. *What was it with his wife Laura? What had happened to their marriage? Could it be that Ben was still in love with Laura? Was still hoping for reconciliation?*

Cassie stood before the damaged wall, looking wistfully at the tattered framing and bits of plaster still clinging to what was left of the wall. She wondered about buying some calico and pinning it to the ceiling to hide the damage. *Maybe Rose and the girls could paint a quick mural on the calico? That would add character to the place and we could pin unframed art works on it. Hmmm.*

"Cassie, it's time to head off to the funeral – you're goin' aren't ya?" Karen enquired, smiling again at last.

"Yes of course, Rose invited me. Shall we go together? I take it you've been to a Yolngu funeral before?"

"No, not really. I've been to ones in my own country down at Alice. Don't think they'll be too different though. I'll try and explain some of it to you Cassie."

Cassie smiled back, pleased that Karen had worked through her inner gremlins, hoping they could resume the friendly open working relationship they had when Cassie first arrived at Umbakala.

They walked into town after locking the art centre and sharing a friendly sandwich. It was obvious where the funeral was being held. Just behind Rose's house was a large group of Yolngu seated in freshly deposited sand, mostly in the shade of a small group of large gum trees. Beside the house was a makeshift tunnel about thirty feet long barely taller than head height. It was constructed with gum tree saplings with leaves still attached, but now nearly brown and fully dried.

"Oh look, there's Ben and Garrawarra. Let's go and sit with them, I think they should be far enough back from the action." Karen eagerly quickened her step as she sat next to Ben.

"Hi Ben. Hi Garrawarra – is it okay for us to sit this close to the front?"

Garrawarra nodded, his face looked grim today,

"Yo, here okay. No closer."

Cassie sat down beside Karen and looked across at the men, nodding her head in a silent greeting. Ben nodded back and held her gaze for a moment longer than a mere greeting. Cassie blushed and looked away first; this was not the time for meaningful looks. She felt in awe at this occasion. There was a murmur of Yolngu voices in the crowd of painted faces. Some sitting, some standing. Different coloured ochres of the clan colours. A number of men wore headbands, carried spears and had body paint, wearing only shorts for modesty. There was a general air of movement and expectancy – dancers were fidgeting, didgeridoo players were setting in to a space beside the funeral tunnel and the men with clap sticks. Then quite unexpectedly, the clap sticks began their hollow rhythm and some men began the mournful high pitched wailing song. Cassie was mesmerised and sat staring as the didgeridoo players joined in with their hollow trumpeting sounds. She felt the hair on the back of her neck start to rise and tingly all over her body. She looked across at Karen and Ben. Ben had goose bumps over his arms – and he was looking at her. Karen had jostled so that her leg was pressed against Ben. Cassie looked away to see Rose get up from the sand and walk to an open space together with a large group of women dancers. Ben leaned forward and looked back at Karen and Cassie, including them both, he said, almost whispering,

"I've been watching them practice their ceremony in the evenings at Garrawarra's place. They are amazing!"

They fell silent, as the women rhythmically shuffled their feet in the sand. *No other dance in the world is anything like this,* thought Cassie. Some of the arm movements were almost like a simulation of rocking a baby, some almost like Polynesian arm and finger gestures, but nothing she had read or seen had prepared Cassie for this spectacle.

The dances lasted for a few minutes, then suddenly stopped. The story was told in the dancing and they returned to their places before another group rose and told another story in song and dance. After about an hour, a new drama unfolded. Some of the women, including Rose, began to wail and scream. Some threw themselves to the ground and threw sand at themselves, signifying some obvious grief. One woman had an old biscuit tin and she was hitting her body and legs while mournfully crying and throwing herself to the ground in apparent despair. Yolngu men, anointed warriors, began milling at the entrance to the bush tomb, appearing to remonstrate and talking to the wailing women. Cassie was deeply moved by the theatre of death, her eyes welled up as she felt the pain of her friend Rose. She could not even contemplate what it would be like to lose either of her parents.

After what seemed like hours of singing, dancing and wailing, the Fijian minister appeared in his black trousers, white shirt and dog collar. Clasping a Bible, he spoke briefly in Yolngu language, while everyone sat and listened in silence. Then the choir from church started singing a mournful Yolngu hymn. Tears streamed down Cassie's cheeks, suppressing sobs that were close. This moment had completely overwhelmed her. Karen sat quietly, knowingly, between Cassie and Ben, but found herself frowning as Ben reached past her and handed a handkerchief to Cassie.

Before long, a white troopy began to reverse toward the tomb. Back doors were opened and after another long period of theatre by the mourners, some men emerged from the tunnel carrying a body wrapped in cloth. *Almost like an Egyptian mummy*, thought Cassie. It wasn't long before the troopy drove off slowly followed by a walking procession of Yolngu. They were going to the cemetery, where Betty Gundwarri would be laid to rest.

Ben woke earlier than usual this particular Saturday. He was keen to have his boat repaired but anxious that a woman was going to do it. He had only taken up sailing in recent years after he had met Laura. Up to now, he had only worked on minor fibreglass repair jobs, but at least he had some understanding of the principles of working with resins.

After a light breakfast, Ben busied himself, preparing for the work that would be done, removing some of the teak lining panels from the inside. Two of them were cracked, but not splintered so he set about gluing and cramping them on the deck. They would be ready to re-fit the next day if necessary. Next he removed the lounge cushions and dining table, so Cassie would have good access to repair the main wall of the hull.

"You awake Ben?" came Mario's gruff voice as he noisily dropped a resin tin and box of materials on the dock.

"Been up for ages Mario – not like you to be up with the birds?" Mario grinned at Ben – unconvincing friendliness.

"Yeah, well. Here's the stuff Cassie ordered – the invoice is in the box. You sure you want a sheila to fix your boat for you? I could do the job next week if you want. It'll cost you though, that's a fair old crack in your hull."

"No thanks Mario, I'll take my chances with Cassie. Anyway, she broke it; she can fix it – law of the bush."

"Alright then but don't come cryin' to me if it's a mess. Tell me though, what's between you and Cassie? I mean, she was comin' onto me, now she's trying to crack onto you man – I reckon she's a tease ..."

Ben looked at him pitifully, not knowing quite what to say to Mario. Mario had after all spent two nights with Cassie, but he hadn't seen any evidence of flirty behaviour from Cassie. Somehow, feelings of protectiveness rose up in Ben as he considered his reply to Mario.

"Look mate, she's not one of your nurses who needs to have a bloke for the sake of having a bloke." His voice quietened, tone more gentle, "She's got integrity Mario. She's different to other women who come up here."

Before Mario could reply, both their heads turned to the sound of footsteps on the end of the wharf. Cassie had arrived carrying a small cool box, dressed in paint stained shorts and frayed vest. They both watched intently, silently, as Cassie's tanned legs walked confidently toward them. Only Ben and Cassie were smiling.

"Good morning boys – is that the stuff Mario?"

"Sure is. You can fix me up any time – gotta go, got fish to catch, see ya later." For once Mario did not walk brashly, his steps unconvincing and head down as he headed back to the boatyard. Cassie looked into Ben's eyes as her smile widened, almost without her knowing. She could feel her heart start to pound in her chest. *I must relax, how can I do this work with my hands shaking? If he was interested he'd have shown it by now? Besides, he's just a friend.* Ben reached out a hand to help Cassie on board. He chuckled to himself at the irony, but his mother had taught him to open doors and to stand up when a woman walked into the room. He was oblivious to the tremble in Cassie's hand. A calm suddenly came between them as Cassie stepped aboard. They each felt a strange familiarity, as if they were long-time friends, each wanting to know even more about the other, yet each wary, like cats sizing up their prey. They sat in the cockpit as Cassie broke the delicious tension that was heavy in the air.

"I brought some lunch. Hope you like cold chicken legs and salad"

"Okay! Let's eat now!"

"Slow down fella – we've got a boat to fix!"

It wasn't long before they had unpacked the resin and repair materials. Ben marvelled at Cassie's speed and efficiency as she collected rags, brushes, mixing and washing buckets from Serendipity. They were more relaxed now, as they brought their heads together and Cassie revealed her repair plan. She was somewhat surprised at how easily Ben agreed to the work plan and how eager he was to learn, with no apparent ego problems, admitting his own inexperience with resin. Ben cut away the damaged fibreglass as Cassie prepared the base matt for the resin to impregnate. Together, they secured it in place then Cassie slowly applied the first layer of resin by brush. Ben made some tea and baked some scones, which were ready just as Cassie finished glassing.

"Mmm, you'd make someone a good husband – can you clean as well?"
Ben did not reply but looked out to sea without smiling.

"I'm sorry Ben. I didn't mean that to come out the way it did. I just forgot you were married."

"In a way I am, in a way I'm not; but can we change the subject please? Maybe one day Cassie – one day."
There was an uncomfortable silence as they sipped on their tea and munched on fresh scones and strawberry jam. The shade from Ben's canvas bimini provided a welcome relief, the ever hot sun and blue sky looking down on their helplessness.

"What did you think of Rose's mum's funeral Cassie? Have you seen anything like that before?" Ben struggled to find some neutral ground.

"I couldn't believe it. It was so moving – there was so much passion and emotion. You know, my mother was always worried that I didn't cry. As a little girl, if I skinned my knee, apparently I wouldn't cry – just grimaced as mom put on the disinfectant. Yet, when I saw Rose and her grief, I just couldn't stop myself. Thanks by the way for your handkerchief, I'll return it to you clean." Cassie felt a slight welling in her eyes now, as she remembered yesterday's ceremony. "I'm sorry," she sniffed, "I don't know why I'm upset. Maybe it's all this stuff with Dumatja." She felt Ben's warm hand touch her arm for comfort. She suddenly wanted him to hold her, to rest her head against his broad shoulder. She wanted to feel safe and secure in the arms of this gentle man. Nonetheless there was something about Ben she was unsure of. There was still uncertainty. She had seen him angry that first day they met and he seemed unforgiving. Was there another side to Ben that she was unable to feel? Could she trust him not to turn again? Just then, she melted, as Ben gently put an arm around Cassie's shoulder as they sat beside each other. His other hand reached out for her hand which she willingly surrendered as she rested her head against the muscles of his shoulder. They sat quietly for what seemed like an eternity, basking in the mellow rocking of the boat; basking in the sheer joy and delight of each other as a warm glow overtook them. Like a winter fire in a snow covered cabin, they warmed themselves in each other's aura – neither wanting the moment to end.

The cooling breeze from the ocean gently flicked wisps of Cassie's dark hair, tickling Ben's forearm. He smiled. The smile turned into a giggle, making Cassie sit up. He looked up into Ben's eyes smiling –

eyebrows raised.

"Your hair; it's tickling. Come on, this isn't getting my boat fixed. Must be time for the next coat!"

Ben unexpectedly playfully, tickled Cassie's waist. It was her turn to giggle as she tried to squirm away from this intimacy.

"You'd better stop this," laughed Cassie. "Don't forget I can beat you at arm wrestling – could easily throw you overboard you know!"

"Oops – sorry, forgot about that." Immediately withdrawing his hands, he held up his palms in mock surrender as Cassie climbed backwards down the hatch-way; her mouth grinning while their eyes stayed locked in an embrace.

As the day and the work progressed, Ben became more and more pleased and satisfied that the repair job would be of a high quality. Cassie became more confident with each layer of resin, neither minding each other's sweating bodies as they focussed on the work, Ben mixing resin batches, Cassie applying it to the hull deftly and expertly. They played in the heat of the day at lunch time like two children in a sand box laughing and joking as they gnawed on cool chicken legs and gulped down light beer followed by orange juice,. That night after dinner, they played Scrabble, their work complete but both reluctant to say goodbye. The tension once more built between them like thunderclouds on a hot summer's day. There was that sometimes inescapable hesitation between a man and a woman; the friendship, the laughter, the closeness of their eager bodies, neither wanting to break the web that had ensnared, yet each holding something back. As they tiptoed sensitively around each other's boundaries, they quietly packed up the Scrabble and sipped on the last of the wine. The stars shouted their brightness in the black sky; the distant evensong of the Yolngu in mourning could be heard faintly in the trees and the hillside.

"I'd better be going now Ben. Thanks for a lovely evening, I just love Scrabble – don't suppose you play chess?"

"Arm wrestling, Scrabble, I suppose you want to thrash me at chess too!" Ben smiled, a broad grin, as he took hold of her hands. Cassie trembled in the tropical air as Ben moved his smiling lips closer to Cassie's. She was uncertain, faltering. She felt vulnerable. She could resist James – she could resist Mario, but could she resist this man? He smelled of soap and pheromones as she felt a sudden weakness in her legs. Then bit by bit, Ben released her hands and put his arms around Cassie, pulling her snugly into his body. She felt his muscles and masculinity as she nestled her head against his shoulder. He kissed her hair and tasted the apple blossoms and sweet ambrosia of a beautiful woman. His fingers ran tenderly through her hair, gently pulling her head even closer to his chest and shoulders. His other hand sent an electric charge through her as he soothingly massaged the aching muscles in her back.

The embrace seemed to last forever, the cool evening doing nothing to cool this new heat. Eventually, Ben pulled away, but held onto Cassie's shoulders as he kissed her slowly on both cheeks.

"You'd better go before I do something we might both regret," said Ben quietly, barely more than a whisper.

Cassie arrived at work on Monday feeling unusually serene and peaceful. The work with Ben had gone better than she had expected and soon they would be able to apply the final finishing gel-coat on the outside of the hull, ready to cut and polish back to a shiny finish. Her muscles still ached but she felt satisfied with the work that they had done. After church on Sunday, Rose had invited her to share lunch with her family and to observe more ceremony as the traditional funeral for her mother continued on during the week. Cassie noted that Dumatja had not made an appearance even though the rest of the village seemed to come and go at different times, taking part in the singing and dancing or just sitting in the sand as a show of respect. An unexpected wave of fear passed through her stomach as she thought of Dumatja again.

For the first time, Cassie had the art centre to herself. Karen had called in sick. Cassie enjoyed the contact with the customers and even though there were only four couples today, they each spent a tidy amount. Cassie was pleased that the month's sales had already exceeded last year's figures. She hoped Karen's stomach complaint would be better by tomorrow so they could do more work toward the Garma Festival.

The day had flown so quickly, Cassie did not notice the time. It was five o'clock when there was a loud knock at the door and Cassie was clenched by fear.

"Hello – you still here Cassie?"
Relieved to hear his voice, Cassie quickly ran to the entrance as Ben stepped into the cool art centre. Covered in dust and sweat, he was carrying a carpenter's tool box. He wore an extra wide grin when he saw Cassie's look of surprise, almost astonishment.

"I came to fix that wall of yours. Figured you might need it for Garma, so I'll come every day after work till it's finished."

"Oh Ben ..." was all Cassie could say as she put her arms around Ben's neck and pecked him on the lips, bouncing up and down with glee. A shocked Ben stood open-mouthed as Cassie skipped away, waving him to follow her into the main exhibition room.

In the first hour, Ben had torn down the last of the termite eaten framing along with Cassie's help. Cassie had slipped into a pair of work jeans and shirt she had stored at the art centre and together they relived the joy of the team work they had shared at Ben's boat. While Ben did the more serious demolition work, Cassie carried the rubble out into the truck after she had finished neatly stacking the framing timber Ben had collected for the job.

"Cypress, see – white ants won't eat this stuff," said Ben gleefully, holding up the tough native timber.

"Ben, you don't know what it means to me and the Yolngu artists. We can really start to promote the works properly now."

No sooner had Cassie shown her joy and thanked Ben, when there was a loud cracking noise at the front door. They both turned as a dull thud followed and an angry Yolngu voice spat out staccato curses. It was Dumatja holding an axe in his hands as he stood in the middle of the room staring an evil stare at Cassie.

"You woman – bad story for art centre." He staggered slightly, knuckles gripping the axe tightly in front of his chest. Ben and Cassie both noticed the drugged glaze in his eyes mixed with a madness neither could recognise. "You – must leave Umbakala now!" He raised the axe and took one step forward. In one neat movement, Ben picked up a piece of timber and stepped in front of Cassie. He moved slowly toward Dumatja and stopped well out of reach of the axe. Dumatja lowered the axe and pointed a bony finger at Ben as he cursed an eerie throaty jumble of Yolngu sounds. "Marrtji, wandi dhipungur wangangur, gatjuwuy!" He backed toward the door, all the time pointing and cursing before finally, he stepped outside and was gone.

9   The Curse

Cassie was still shaking when Ben dropped the piece of wood he was holding, his shiny knight's sword.

"Are you alright Cassie?" He put his arms around her – a fatherly hug; loving and protective. He kissed the top of her head when she did not answer and pulled her even closer. "It's okay, it's okay – he's gone now."

"I-I'm scared Ben. He had an axe. Did he want to kill me or was he just trying to frighten me?"

"I think he was just trying to scare you. He said he wanted you to leave, remember?"

"Well, he's frightened me alright. And leave? That's just what I want to do; right now."

"You're safe with me Cassie. I don't think you should be alone at the moment. I know what we need to do. Will you stay with me while we try to sort this out?"

"I'm not leaving your side, Ben Brogan. Do you think we should call the police?"

"I was just going to call Mike first; he has all the police contacts in Nhulunbuy. I reckon he'll have to act this time with the position he's in."
Ben rang the office, then Mike's home number; there was no answer at either place.

"Come on Cassie, let's go up to the council office and see what's happened to him."
They were able to lock the art centre, the front door was solid hardwood and the axe mark of Dumatja's reminder, was not sufficient to damage the door badly.

As they drove along the dirt road toward the council building, Ben kept hold of Cassie's hand, casting concerned glances toward her every so often. Cassie felt tense but safe with this man. She was able to see a side of Ben she did not know existed. He had been so calm and in control in that life and death situation. A situation where he could have been killed – they both could have been killed. Now he was holding her hand tenderly, caring for her like no man had ever done before. Could he be her knight in shining armour? She knew he cared, but he was still married – wasn't he?

Nearing the building, they could see the empty space where Mike's car was usually parked, but Charlie Alanja's troopy was parked out the front. In the distance they could see a commotion in front of the general store. People were milling, and some were laughing.

"Come on, Alanja's inside, let's tell him what happened."

For once the security lock was set. Ben keyed in the numbers and they went inside. Djingala and two other women were huddled in the reception area with worried looks on their faces. Djingala spoke, "Mike took off to Darwin. Dumatja was looking for him."

"Thanks Djingala, is Alanja here?"

"Yo, he and Bulangi in board room."

They stepped across the corridor and through the double doors of the meeting room. The two Yolngu councillors were standing at the window, smoking and looking out toward the general store. Alanja gave a nervous laugh and smiled at Ben and Cassie as they entered the room.

"Hello Ben. Cassie. You hear what happen in town?"

"Was it something to do with George Dumatja?"

"Yo, he come here with axe looking for Mike. Mike hide in toilet, ha, ha, ha. Then Dumatja go to store and put curse on store."

"He cursed the store?"

"Yo, store not open now till curse removed."

"So who can take this curse off the store?"

"Only Dumatja or old man from clan. Dumatja gone walkabout – we get Dumatja father to take off curse."

Cassie sank down in a seat, holding her head in her hands; it had started to throb. She could not believe this was happening. *Axes, curses; what next?*

"Cassie okay Ben?" asked Bulangi with a concerned look on his face.

"She's scared Bulangi. Dumatja just put an axe into the art centre door and threatened Cassie with it – told her to leave Umbakala."

The two Yolngu men looked at each other, then at Ben and Cassie, before sitting down and engaging in animated conversation in Yolngu language. Ben sat down and put an arm around Cassie's shoulders before he again had an opportunity to speak.

"I want to ring the police Alanja, before Dumatja kills someone."

"Won't do no good Ben. Unless someone killed, police don't care. They say this Yolngu matter, not police matter."

"But he threatened Cassie. He had an axe!"

They sat silently for a while before Ben spoke again.

"Can't you do something? What about Yolngu traditional law? What about the other clan leaders?"

"Yo Ben. We get clan leader's meeting soon." Alanja paused and then added, "You know Ben, when Dumatja come to council ask for money, if I say no, I have to fight him. I scared too Ben. I old man – Dumatja have powerful magic."

"What about us Alanja? Do you think we'll be safe on our boats for the moment?"

"Yo Ben. Dumatja leave village for long time now. He have shame. Maybe next month before return."

"Even so, I don't think Cassie should be staying in her house any more. Come on Cassie, let's get your things, you're staying on my boat tonight."

As they walked with determination from the council offices, Cassie shared an observation with Ben.

"Dumatja seems to have a lot of people frightened. He has me scared, then there's Mike and even Alanja! He's even got the senior clan leaders and council president scared, Ben. He's terrorising the whole community and it doesn't look like anyone can do anything about it."

"I know Cassie, but let's just take one step at a time. I know that running away doesn't solve your problems. Somehow we need to take a stand. I believe we should try to work this out with the senior men. I reckon Alanja and Bulangi are the key to this."

Ben pulled up to the gate of Casssie's house. Cassie stepped out of the truck to open the gate.
"Will you come in Ben while I grab some things?" She wasn't going to argue with him about not staying in her house. She could think of better ways to die than being axed in her sleep.

They walked up the steps of the verandah and were jolted to a stop when the front door began to open, slowly. Ben took a step forward in front of Cassie. It was Rose wearing a worried frown on her brow.

"You no stay here Cassie – bad magic here."

"What do you mean Rose?"

Rose did not have to answer. They went into the once clean house and were met with a vile smell. The first thing they saw was the human faeces in the middle of the living room. Despite the screens, a few blow flies had made their way in and were hovering round their prize. On the walls was something even more shocking. Cassie gasped as she put a hand up to her mouth and started to back away from the wall. She stopped when she bumped into Ben, who immediately put his arms round her once again. Cassie felt dazed and confused at the horror, but somehow she also felt comforted and almost at peace, tucked away inside a pair of strong arms. Painted on the wall in front of her was the shape of a crocodile and some dots and strokes that were not recognisable. It looked like blood. Thick drops of dark red liquid had run in places toward the floor, and dried, underlining this macabre artwork. Ben and Cassie turned to Rose as one, hoping for an explanation.

"You must go Cassie. I clean up mess, but house cursed. Crocodile Dumatja's clan totem. Only Dumatja clan can take away curse."

"I'm going to stay on my boat. Rose, thank you for everything. Will you be okay here on your own?"

"I be alright, no worry about me."

"Will you come to the art centre in the morning so we can talk about this?"

"Yo Miss Cassie. Tomorrow – but you go now – okay?"

Cassie quickly packed some clothes and personal items in a soft bag while Ben helped Rose clean the living room floor under the watchful eye of the crocodile curse. It wasn't long before they drove down to the docks and the safety of their floating homes. They did not say much, each captured in their own thoughts re-living the dramas of the afternoon. *Would life be ever peaceful in Umbakala?* Thought Cassie; then she pictured Henry Garrawarra and the happy picture of his family, his wife and children. Was this village just a microcosm of the rest of the world – the struggle between good and evil? Pockets of elusive happiness here and there?

Ben carried Cassie's bag in one hand and put his other arm around her waist as they walked slowly down the dock.

"I think you should stay on my boat tonight Cassie, just in case."

"I'll be okay on Serendipity Ben, you heard what Alanja said; Dumatja's gone walkabout and should be gone for some time."

"That's right, *should* be gone. I'm not talking no for an answer Miss Cassie, even at the risk of getting thrown overboard by you!"

Cassie laughed at the suggestion and remembered their earlier light hearted conversation. She felt safe with Ben and sure he could be trusted; trusted to protect her life, trusted to look after her honour.

"Okay Ben. Anyway, I'm too exhausted to fight with you. Strange how tiring death threats and curses are – oh, do you think the curse is starting to take effect? I mean, do you think it starts with tiredness till eventually you have no energy left to live?"

It was Ben's turn to laugh as he placed Cassie's bag on board and held out his hand to her.

"I've read a little about aboriginal witch doctors pointing the bone at someone and that person eventually dies, but I reckon it's just about the power of suggestion; that person has to believe they are going to die. I think Haitian black magic might be something similar. Anyway, it can't possibly work on you; you're a strong willed child!"

"Me? Look who's talking; Mr '*I'm not paid to do odd jobs at the art centre,*' Brogan."

"Ha, ha, ha – okay, you're right, we're both strong willed children. We both fit the definition. By the way, I once read a book on the topic."

"Strong willed children?"

"Yep, the theme and the title was something like, '*You can't make me, but I can be persuaded.*' I reckon if we were tested, we'd both get high scores."

"Hey Ben, just to change the subject, I wasn't hungry a minute ago, but now I wouldn't mind a light snack. How about some crackers and cheese with a bit of fruit?"

The sun was almost below the rim of the ocean and had cast a pink plume of gossamer netting in the surrounding sky. They sat in the cockpit side by side nibbling on crackers and sipping on chilled Chablis. The wine seemed as much out of place as they were, but it was a comforting reminder of another culture, of romantic hillsides and French peasants from another era crushing grapes in oak vats, while mandolins played love songs under shady elm trees. Conversation moved to childhood stories, silly stories that enabled them to laugh at themselves; stories that took them away from the terrible dilemmas that faced them tomorrow, the day after or in the weeks to come.

"I wonder where we'll be this time next year Ben?"

"I reckon I'll still be here. I've never had so much real purpose in my work before. This is not just about putting a roof over people's heads, it's about changing people's lives for the better."

"I know what you mean. I feel it too with the art centre. I mean, potentially, the Yolngu artists could make a reasonable living from their art – no more sit-down money."

"There's just one major problem – George Dumatja."

"Don't forget about Mike, although his little embezzling tricks don't seem as important now. Anyway, I'm determined to go to work tomorrow. Karen and I can just lock the doors and pretend we're not there, unless of course a tourist comes with a pocket full of money. We'll let *them* in."

"I've been thinking Cassie. We can't have the concrete pour until Wednesday, so I'll just bring the boys over tomorrow and we can finish the wall and dig up the sewerage lines at the same time. It'll be good to keep them busy. With numbers, I reckon we might be able to finish both jobs."

"Are you sure? That's so sweet of you; I don't know how I can ever thank you for all you've done for me."

"I'm just happy to help. I know we got off on the wrong foot with each other, but we're friends now – right?"

"Surely friends," laughed Cassie, her heart pounding as they embraced. She felt the rough stubble of his cheek against hers, felt the strength in his arms. Was this love? She was tired of resisting her urges, her natural desires, but this man was not available. Cassie inwardly fought her battle as Ben gently stroked her hair, sending shivers down the back of her neck, then on to her spine. She trembled and let out a quiet groan, then hoped that it had sounded like a sigh. She did not want to lead him on; it was up to him to tell her if he wanted her, if he was available to want her. She felt she must hold back and not surrender, but it was getting harder as she allowed herself to melt into the moment, to melt into the arms of this beautiful man.

Ben looked down at the gorgeous sleeping woman in his arms. He had completely lost track of the time as they sat entwined, the stars above them rocking gently in the Arafura swell. Cassie looked so peaceful with her eyes closed, no sound of breathing, just the rising and falling of her soft breasts sheltering beneath the sheer cotton blouse. It was not the first time he denied his own arousal; he wanted to hold her and never let her go, but how could he? How could he betray Laura? He decided to try and carry Cassie below deck; to see if he could put her to bed without waking her. He knew she needed rest tonight. She looked helpless and vulnerable as she sheltered her head in his left shoulder and he easily picked her up like she was a small child. She stirred slightly and mumbled incoherently as she put one arm around Ben's neck and shoulder. Slowly, deliberately, he stepped down the hatchway and gently placed her on the forward v-berth. A light, warm breeze was blowing – no blankets needed. Cassie turned in her sleep and rolled over onto her side and then lay still and quiet as Ben delicately loosened the straps of her sandals and slowly removed each one, careful not to wake her. He stared, a long loving stare at Cassie's legs, her tanned skin barely lit up by the lounge cabin light. He was wide awake as he sat, a silent sentinel, feeling such happiness in the presence of this woman, happiness he felt he did not deserve – she deserved better than him.

Eventually, tiredness began to overtake him. He kissed Cassie's sleeping feet, one after the other, like a mother might kiss a baby before he curled up on the settee in the galley. A kiss of innocence – a kiss of tender love.

The next morning, Ben drove Cassie to the art centre and after asking her again to promise that she would lock the door, drove off to the building site to reveal the changed work plan for the day to Garrawarra and the men. They were all enthusiastic. Cassie and Ben had both earned their respect and they were keen to help her with the art centre. Cassie woke after the sun was fully up and was surprised, firstly by how well she had slept and then by Ben's comatose body on the berth by the galley. She had looked at Ben breathing deeply, his body twisted in awkward angles on the narrow bed. Drawn by an urge of gratitude or love – she wasn't sure – she kissed him on his cheek. The even thicker stubble felt like pins on her lips, but she did not mind, a knight deserved at least one kiss from the rescued princess. A princess who would cook her knight a hearty breakfast.

Cassie shuddered as she locked the front door of the art centre behind her. The deep gouge of the axe mark was a reminder of yesterday's chilling encounter with Dumatja. She grabbed a broom and spent a long time sweeping the remaining debris and demolition dust from the two galleries where the joining wall had once stood. Cleaning the gallery was normally Karen's job, but Cassie felt the need to purge some of her nervous energy – this was not the time to sit in front of the computer doing administration work. She was calm when she heard a firm knock at the door, knowing it would be either Ben or Karen. Carrying a stool over to the high gallery window, she stepped up to see who was at the door. It was Karen.

"Hi Karen, glad you're in early, we've got a lot to talk about."

"You don't mean about Dumatja cursing the store? Everyone's talkin' about it."

"No – er, I mean that and the other things Dumatja's done. Come on, I'll make us some coffee. We can talk in my office." Cassie looked nervous, a furrow on her brow as she unfolded yesterday's events to Karen. As she was talking she sensed Karen become more uneasy, wringing her hands together tightly as she spoke and rubbing her eye vigorously with the back of her hand. When she had finished, Cassie put her hand on Karen's arm. "Are you okay, Karen, you're shaking?"

"I-I'm scared Cassie. He's evil that bloke – I know what he can do to a woman." Without warning Karen started to cry, clutching her face with both hands – sobs coming uncontrollably in bursts as she rocked backwards and forwards in her chair. Cassie put a consoling arm around Karen.

"It's alright Karen, we're safe. Ben and the men will be here any minute to fix the wall. Dumatja can't hurt us – it's alright."

"I'm not cryin' about that. It's, it's – I can't talk about it. Gary couldn't save me; he didn't even try to help. 'E was just too strong." She continued to weep as Cassie encircled Karen in her arms, feeling the tears wet on her shoulder.

"Sometimes it helps to talk about things. Karen you can trust me – I might be able to help."

"No one can help. I was s-so frightened and all because Gary couldn't keep his willy in his pants."

"What do you mean? Are you talking about the time you told me

Gary was having sex with some of the girls from Dumatja's clan?"

"The stupid idiot – it was all his fault."

"*What* was his fault Karen? What happened to you?"

"The clan had to get even. Dumatja had to get revenge." Karen sniffed and took a deep breath before continuing. "He told me we were going to get ochre for painting. I didn't want to get into the car, but something made me – like I was powerless to refuse him."

"You mean Dumatja? Karen; he made you get into his car?"

"Y-yes. He drove me to the beach – to that creek where that big crocodile lives. He told me I had a choice. I could either have sex with him in the sand under the mangroves, it was low tide you see – or – he said he would tie me to the mangroves for the croc. The croc comes back in with the tide Cassie ..." She sobbed even harder when there was another knock at the door. Cassie had heard the truck pull up a minute before. It had to be Ben.

"Just wait a minute Karen, it's Ben. I have to let him in. Don't worry, I'll shut the door. I won't let anyone see you like this."

After letting Ben and his co-workers in, Cassie quickly returned, after briefly explaining to Ben that Karen was upset - a woman thing. Ben had not asked for further explanations.

Karen was trying to compose herself when Cassie closed the office door behind her. She saw how red Karen's eyes were as she once more put her arms around Karen, stroking her back – woman consoling woman.

"What happened then Karen? Did you tell the police?"

"No. Dumatja said if I told anyone, the police, he'd tell them about Gary screwin' the fifteen year olds. Said Gary would go to gaol. Told me he knew about white man's laws."

"Did you tell Gary what happened?"

"Didn't have to. Somehow he musta known – must've been told by someone. When I got back to town, 'e was gone – didn't even take all his stuff – just shot through. Never heard from 'im again."

"Oh Karen, you must have been devastated!"

"Never been so alone in me life. No one to talk to, no one to help me. I just curled up in me bed and cried – don't know how long – musta been days, I just wanted to die Cassie. Then Rose found me. She's like a mother to me, Rose. She didn't say much. She held me, she sang to me – cleaned me up, fed me. Got me back up again. Didn't think I could ever face that evil bastard again Cassie – but I did."

"You're so brave Karen. I never would have guessed."

"Me? You're pretty brave too Cassie. You're still 'ere after 'e held you up against the wall by the throat."

"That was nothing compared to what you've been through. I'm glad you told me all this Karen. You know, together, I think we make a pretty tough team!" Karen laughed a nervous laugh as they ended the hug, facing each other and holding hands. Just then, there was a knock at the door and Rose walked in. "Hello Rose, Karen just told me about what Dumatja did to her." Tears immediately rolled down Rose's black face as she walked over to where Karen and Cassie were standing. She put an arm around each woman and started singing. To Cassie it sounded like a lullaby; a Yolngu lullaby. Maybe it was a song that had comforted thousands of Yolngu babies over the centuries? Maybe it was a song just to comfort them?

The work on the building seemed to proceed quickly. By mid-morning, one group of men had built a new wall frame and another had dug a large trench behind the art centre, exposing the clay sewerage pipes. Then the whole group came together and lifted the frame into place with Ben barking orders and cracking jokes with Garrawarra as they nailed it into place. In the meantime, the women had driven to the store hoping the curse had been lifted. Luckily trading was back to normal and they were able to buy flour and eggs and food for lunch. The cake was baked and layered with jam, just as the last nail went into place securing the new wall. Cassie thought it was like a scene from a barn raising, where families and friends all gathered to work and feast together to celebrate their building success.

They had all gathered on the floor of the main gallery, surrounded by mugs of tea and slices of cake on paper plates, laughing and joking as if no one had a care in the world, when Ben rose to his feet and proposed a toast.

"To Yolngu art! May the world one day see the beauty of Yolngu traditions."

No sooner had they all drunk the toast, when Cassie stood up next to Ben, clinking her mug against his, her smiling eyes lingering and probing into the depths of his.

"To the Yolngu building team! May they build many beautiful houses in Umbakala."

The day continued – hard work and celebration. Wall sheeting and plumbing parts were picked up from the storage shed, tree roots were cleared from the sewer pipe and the wall was clad, all the time the buzz of energy continued.

The last of the workers left the art centre late, leaving Cassie and Ben to lock up. Cassie looked closely at the wooden block Ben had skilfully inserted into the axe damage. She hoped that this might be a sign; a sign that whatever it was that Dumatja did could be fixed. She hoped that all his evil could be neutralised, just like that door.

"This was such a wonderful day Ben, all thanks to you," said Cassie, as they strolled along the dock towards their two sloops, gleaming gold in the last light of the day.

"Couldn't have done it without you and your support crew; that cake for smoko was a stroke of genius, the boys really liked that. By the way, what's wrong with Karen, her eyes were so red – looked like she'd been crying?"

"I'm not sure I should tell you Ben. It's Karen's story. Please don't tell her I told you. It's to do with Dumatja."

"Dumatja? What; did he do something to Karen?"

Cassie told Ben the whole story about Dumatja's revenge and how he had effectively raped Karen.

"I've read that rape is mostly about power rather than sexual gratification. Looks like he's got power over the community, Mike and even council. But he hasn't got power over us. It must be killing him that we're still here. I think we have to be careful, a bloke like that isn't going to just roll over and go away."

"You're right Ben, what do you suggest we do?"

Before he could answer, Mario's ute had driven up to the end of the dock. Mario got out and walked over to them as they stood next to Serendipity.

"G'day guys, I heard there's been a bit of trouble with Dumatja?"

"Nothing Ben couldn't handle," said Cassie proudly.

"Look, don't underestimate this guy. Remember, I grew up here, I know some of the bad stuff he's done. Remember my eighteen year old Yolngu friend and how he died for no obvious reason? Have you heard what he did to Karen?"

"We know about that Mario and we *are* worried."

"Yeah, but at the end of the day, he's just one bloke," said Ben sounding more confident than he felt.

"Look, all I can say is, I think you should both leave as soon as possible. Cassie, just give me a couple of days to fix your rudder. I'll do it for nothing, then you just high tail it out of here. In the meantime, you can stay at my place; I've got a spare bunk."

"She's staying with me on my boat," said Ben as he looked toward Cassie for confirmation.

"Thanks – both of you – you've both been very kind, but I'm going to stay on Serendipity. I need my own space to think things through. I don't want to just run away, but I don't want to be killed either." Cassie turned and quickly stepped aboard her boat and disappeared down below, leaving Ben and Mario staring after her, mouths open.

10   The Yacht Race

Cassie woke the next morning to the sound of a kookaburra laughing. The cacophony of sounds alarmed her in her half sleep, then she smiled as she rubbed her eyes and pictured a smiling beaked native bird sitting in a nearby gum tree. She had not slept well, waking often to look at the time, aware of the slightest hushed bush noises. She was jumpy and had a good reason to be. Somewhere out in the bush was a deranged and angry Yolngu man who wanted rid of her, who certainly wasn't going to have a white woman at the art centre with any authority over him. Cassie had looked over the historical accounts that day with Lesley's help and had scrutinised the twelve month period where Dumatja had been appointed the art centre manager. The books showed the centre had been completely in the red; it was clear that Dumatja just took money out when it suited him. She wondered if he either did not understand balanda business or simply did not care? Either way, picking up the pieces was challenging and satisfying and Cassie felt she was starting to achieve results. *If only somehow I could continue with this job – If only Dumatja could be taken out of the picture so Yolngu, Umbakala art could be a real success in the art world.*

She sat quietly as Ben drove them up the hill toward the art centre.

"Cassie, I'll leave my mobile phone on all day today. I want you to ring me straight away if there's any trouble."

"I will, I promise." Cassie looked over serenely, smiling and put a hand on Ben's arm. Ben immediately felt alive, happier that Cassie had made some effort to connect with him again. He was confused after last night, when Cassie seemed to just cut him off and storm off into Serendipity. He wanted to care for her, to protect her, but she was so strong willed, so independent. *Just like Laura,* he thought, as they arrived at the art centre.

"Listen, we'll finish the concrete pour by lunch time. I can come over and help you paint the walls and tidy up some of the trim this afternoon if that's okay Cassie?"

"I'd like that Ben. See you later."

Ben watched as she disappeared behind the locked door of the art centre. He looked all through the surrounding bush before driving off to the building site, not really expecting to see Dumatja crouching in ambush, but he just felt a sudden uneasiness; worry for Cassie. He was comforted by the thought that she was less than one hundred metres away from the building site – he could be at the art centre in minutes, seconds if he had to.

The concrete pour was a success. The men stood back in groups chatting as the concrete truck drove off. They were proud of what they had achieved so far and looked forward to starting on the walls in the next few days. A small crowd of old men, women and children began to disperse; some of them shouting out words of praise and encouragement. Ben made sure he thanked and praised every worker individually before gathering them together to talk about the work plans for the next few days. Ben had never experienced such job satisfaction, such raw enthusiasm since he felt the joy of building his first cottage. He was proud to think that Umbakala would soon have a competent building team that could build their own houses and no longer have to just watch outside contractors do it all for them.

When Ben arrived back at the art centre, he stepped up to the door and saw a brass bell hanging outside. Finding the door locked, he rang the bell and smiled at Cassie's ingenuity with this new security item. He looked over and saw a pair of eyes peeping down at him from the high gallery window – it was Cassie checking him out.

"Hi Ben! Come in, we've got sandwiches ready for you before we start painting."

Ben followed Cassie into Karen's work area which doubled as a distribution spot and lunch room. Karen sat in silence and barely acknowledged Ben's presence. Cassie had openly told Karen that Mario was aware of what had happened to her with Dumatja and how she had told Ben as well, saying that he needed to know what Dumatja was capable of so he could help and protect them if necessary. Karen sat in stony silence staring at the floor while Cassie was talking. Her eyes were wide open.

Lunch was hurried, with Ben doing most of the talking as he proudly described the building work and how quickly the men were learning. As she began tidying the lunch things, Cassie outlined her plans.

"Karen's going to pack a few mail orders this afternoon Ben, while you and I paint the new walls. I've dusted off the rollers and brushes and the paint is here ready to go."

Ben found himself in one room, brush in hand, paint at his feet, while Cassie was in the next room, painting the other side. He decided the mood needed brightening. Lunch had been a sombre affair, so he felt a cheeky urge to take Cassie's mind off the black cloud hanging over the art centre. Painting the wall wouldn't take long, so he started to compose a silly limerick and scrawl it in large bold letters on the raw plasterboard.

'I know a girl called Kookaburra Cassie,
She laughs just like a wee bonnie lassie!
One day she sailed across the sea,
Then smashed a boat and laughed with glee,
It's my friend Cassie from Tallahassee!'

Pleased with his handiwork, Ben put his smiling face round the corner where Cassie was painting.

"Finished! Hey, you've hardly started yours?"

"You have *not* finished – show me!"

Cassie grinned as she brushed past Ben to look at his work. Her hand went up to subdue her giggles as Ben stood back watching her, not knowing what to expect.

"You! You vandal closet poet you!" Cassie spun round and before Ben could react, planted a perfect dab of white paint on the tip of his nose, before jabbing at his shirt, posing as a fencer.

"En guarde you blaggard – prepare to meet thy doom."

Ben laughed, then immediately transformed his brush into a sword, gaining two quick strikes on Cassie's already paint stained shirt.

"Kookaburra am I? Laughed at your smashed boat did I?" She was laughing now as they covered each other with paint splotches, when Ben suddenly ended the fight by grabbing Cassie in a bear hug. He could feel the wet brush on his back as Cassie's arms went around him, he could feel the excitement once again as he held this beautiful woman in his arms. He could see her eyes shyly smiling up at him – she wasn't fighting any longer.

"Did you hear that kookaburra this morning Cassie? Her laugh reminded me of you."

"That raucous cackle? I would have thought I was more like a cooing dove?"

"No – too loud to be a dove. I think I'll have to call you Kookaburra Cassie from now on, or maybe just Kooky? What do you think?"

Cassie melted in Ben's strong arms and as she looked up into his soft brown eyes, she wondered if he was going to kiss her again; after all, it was the art centre where he had kissed her before, so suddenly, so hungrily.

"I think certain closet poets shouldn't give up their day job. So it must have been your poem I found on the floor that day – that day you, er, attacked me."

Ben blushed and released his hold on Cassie. He looked down and shuffled his feet.

"It might have been. You're right, I am a closet poet – don't pretend to be any good at it. It's more like therapy, a hobby really – just a way to express yourself without writing a lot of words."

"Ben, I love that you're a poet – nothing to be ashamed of. Anyway, this isn't getting the walls painted. Thanks for cheering me up, you are quite mad you know."

"Takes one to know one Cassie." Ben smirked, the paint brush still held high in defence, when Cassie stood on tip toes and kissed him lightly on the cheek.

"Come on Buffalo Ben, we've got work to do!"

Cassie worked through the afternoon smiling, pondering Ben's energy and spontaneous silliness. She pulled out the scrap of paper with *that* poem on it. The poem took on a new meaning, now that she knew it had not been written by Mario. *Angelic face, hmm, so he thinks I'm pretty. Voice – loud iron darts; what did he mean by that?*
Her thoughts were suddenly interrupted as a paint splattered Ben poked his head into the doorway of Cassie's office. Cassie looked sheepish as she secretly slipped Ben's poem back into the desk drawer, hoping Ben would not see she had been reading it.

"Cassie, I just have to slip round to the store before we head off. Forgot to tell you, we're going round to Garrawarra's for dinner tonight, we're contributing frozen pizza and I'm just about to pick it up."

"That's very presumptuous of you Ben Brogan, making my dinner arrangements for me like that?"

"You'll be safe that way Cassie and besides, the senior men are meeting tonight to talk about Dumatja. With a bit of luck, they might have some answers to Mr George Dumatja and all the problems he's been causing."

It was still light when they drove through town toward North beach and the cliff top where the clan leaders met on clan business. They drove past Mike's house and the council building; no red car, Mike was still away, perhaps still in hiding?

Approaching Garrawarra's house, they could see the clearing and the lone tree with the ocean behind, where the important tribal business took place. No one was there yet, but two of Garrawarra's boys were throwing their makeshift spears in front of the house. Cassie watched with interest as they stopped their game and ran over to Ben as he stepped out of the car. They each grabbed a leg, giggling and chattering as Ben effortlessly walked along using two boys as legs.

"Namirri Ben, Cassie. You just in time for Balanda barbeque." Garrawarra happily led them onto the verandah of his house where his other children were sitting. Ben handed over his now thawed pizzas and introduced Cassie to Garrawarra's wife.

"Cassie, this is Linda – she's the one responsible for all these kids." He spoke just as two of them ran past squealing at the top of their voices. Linda smiled as she took Cassie's extended hand, before cuffing Ben with a back hander on his arm.

"Not just me – Henry have something to do with making children too."

Cassie felt the peace of being surrounded by their love and warmth. She wondered how there could be such a contrast between a man like Garrawarra and someone like Dumatja – same tribe, same environment.

They sat on the verandah overlooking the bay to the north, as Linda handed out white bread rolls bulging with fat sausages and onions, dripping with tomato sauce. Garrawarra bowed his head and everyone suddenly became quiet as he spoke.

"Let us give thanks ..."

Ben and Cassie were still chatting outside when Garrawarra left them to join the elders gathering under the tree. They could see them sitting round a fire, an eerie light flickering over their distant faces. Cassie felt the clock turn back; back hundreds of years when so called primitive tribes gathered round camp fires and performed their tribal rituals. Ben had just explained how Yolngu people used the evening camp fires as a time for learning. It was a time and place for the Yolngu university where the knowledge, the history, the stories were passed down from generation to generation. Nothing was written – the knowledge was stored in the minds of the men and women. She learnt that they used to have three levels of parliament in ancient Arnhem Land as well as an intellectual language only known and used by the wisest of senior men. Cassie, like Ben, was saddened that this cultural knowledge was being lost; lost to fast foods and western technologies like television and DVD movies; lost to younger generations wearing baseball caps backwards and idolising black American culture, as seen on TV.

As Linda returned after making sure the boys were doing their homework, Cassie and Linda ignored Ben as they got to know one another, chatting about children, clothes and cultural differences. As Ben sat transfixed, staring at the glow of the distant camp fire, he saw Garrawarra get up and walk towards them.

"Ben, you come over now? Old men want talk to you."

"Sure thing, anything I can do to help."

As they walked toward the band of clan leaders, Garrawarra explained that they wanted to hear Ben's account of the Dumatja axe incident. They sat down cross legged in the sand, Ben anxious as he watched the glow of the firelight glinting in the eyes of the eight black men. He felt as if he was in a court of law and about to give evidence. He spoke slowly, delivering all the detail and answering all the questions. Here there was not one lawyer, but eight. Eight wise men who were looking for truth – eight wise men who were looking for justice.

After his eyewitness account, Ben was able to talk about Dumatja holding Cassie up against the wall by the throat, and about the 'art-work' he'd left in her house. He also told them about Karen's experience when she was taken by Dumatja to crocodile creek. Even though they already knew about all three incidents, the old men let him speak until he was finished. Then Alanja spoke.

"Ben - we thank you for talkin' to us now. We want say sorry; sorry that good balanda like you, Cassie and Karen have such troubles, because this man. We know you here help us. We know you good balanda. We now try protect you, old way, Yolngu law way."

"Thank you Alanja. I just want to say that Cassie and I love your people. We are happy to be here and share our knowledge, so that your men can build houses and your artists can share your culture with the world. But we are worried. We're afraid of what Dumatja might do next."

Ben took his leave from the Yolngu tribunal. He walked back to Garrawarra's house alone, where Cassie and Linda were sitting in the dim light of the verandah chatting like old friends, the light flickering with the wings of tiny moths and other insects of the night.

As they drove slowly through the village, past the iridescent lights of televisions in Yolngu houses and the sounds of pop and rap music, Ben told Cassie about the elder's meeting and how they were looking to traditional Yolngu law to deal with Dumatja. When they arrived and walked along the dock to their floating homes, Cassie turned to Ben and posed a question; a question that had been troubling her all day.

"So, how will they punish Dumatja? I mean they don't have any gaols? Are they going to spear him in the leg? Can they banish him from Umbakala? What exactly can they do to protect us from him? Take away his axe?"

They stopped next to Serendipity; Ben turned to face Cassie and took hold of both her hands.

"I don't know. I put some of these questions to Garrawarra, but he said he couldn't say. He said he had a lot to learn about *the law*, but it was an area of secret men's business. These things were just for senior men to know. He did imply though that they even had the death penalty for some offences." Ben did not let Cassie respond, as he moved toward Cassie surrounding her with his arms, enveloping her and taking them both to that place of escape. Their escape was love and friendship and a sharpening of senses that had been hidden and dulled as they tuned into each other's breathing, feeling each other's heartbeat. Cassie felt so ready to be with this man. He did not have to tell her he loved her, she just knew it; could feel it. Yes, she wanted him, but she knew they had much more than lust or the notion of being in love. She knew this had to be the closest she would come to the real thing. She drifted into a warm cloud of desire, her hands clutching at the firmness of Ben's back, her legs weakened as she let herself relax in Ben's arms.

Ben could smell the cherry blossoms in Cassie's hair, could feel the delicious softness of her breasts pressing into his chest, the snugness of her beautiful body nestled against him and in his arms. How could he love two women at the same time? It just did not feel right – he could never stop loving Laura; yet, here was this vibrant stunning woman, so real, so warm, and so loving in his arms right now. He knew he had no right to take her – he would have to be strong, to crush his natural desires to be with Cassie tonight. He felt her surrender in his arms, and yet, he fought the passion, he had to separate his love for this woman from his desire – he had to do this. He first kissed her on the hair above her ear, a light touch of lips; a token of love. He then released his arms and took Cassie by the shoulders, placing his forehead against hers. Smiling down at her, he said,

"Goodnight Kookaburra," as he kissed her slowly and softly, first on one cheek, then the other. Cassie looked up into Ben's latte eyes, her own blue eyes mirroring his love.

"Goodnight Buffalo Ben." They stood that way without saying another word, just lingering in each other's eyes. Finally, Cassie reached to Ben's mouth with her lips and brushed them lightly; the temptation to part her lips was overwhelming, but Cassie resisted. *Not tonight, he needs to sort things out – not tonight.* She quickly turned and with a wave and a warm smile over her shoulder, she disappeared into the depths of Serendipity.

Over the next two weeks, working life for Ben and Cassie took on a routine. Cassie continued to live on Serendipity, sometimes sharing meals with Ben, at other times they kept to their own space. Without talking about it, they both decided to take a step back from each other, yet, every day; Ben would drive Cassie to the art centre, and then drive her home at the end of the day while at times taking her to the store to pick up provisions. They had finished the repairs to Ben's boat and had celebrated with champagne. The surface was not quite as smooth as it had been but it was a good job and Ben found that it did not seem to matter as much. Meanwhile, Cassie, Karen and Rose had all but completed the final preparations for their exhibition at the Garma Festival. The site for the festival was about twenty kilometres away on a flat plateau which overlooked the Gulf of Carpentaria if you could peer through the surrounding gum trees. Most of the tourists and performers would be housed in a tent city adjoining the cleared performance areas and main stage. Two large catering shelters were permanently erected. They were simple structures with bush poles and iron roofs and open to the trade winds and breezes. Cassie looked forward to the week - the promise of Yolngu cultural themes and the chance to share their art works with people from all over the world.

In the week leading up to Garma, Ben had persuaded Cassie to move Serendipity back into the shallow water at high tide. Mario had told him how they could use the dock as careening poles and get access to Cassie's rudder at low tide. Serendipity would rest against the poles built into the wharf, while the keel would wedge itself into the sand. Mario insisted on helping Ben and Cassie to remove what was left of the damaged rudder, and then plug up the hole temporarily before the tide came in. As they examined the remnants of the stainless steel shaft and mangled rudder frame, Mario was quick to make a pronouncement.

"Listen, I can cut the shaft here, weld on a new extension – I've got some pipe the same diameter in the shed, then weld on some ribbing and you can just glass over that. Better than a new one!"

"Do you think we could have it finished by Saturday? I'd like to take Karen, Rose and some of the girls out for a sail before we got to Garma."

"Why not Cassie, I could help with the glassing after work? What do you reckon Mario?" said Ben.

"The sooner the better mate. I still say Cassie has to get out of here as soon as she can. Dumatja won't stay away forever you know!" Mario scowled at Ben as he spoke. He had been uneasy these last few weeks. Cassie even found herself wondering if she had preferred his outrageous flirting to the serious and humourless Mario that he had become. But it was Ben's optimism that changed the mood for Cassie.

"Hey, I've got an idea. Sunday afternoon, I'll take on Garrawarra and his family as crew and we'll race you round the Granites! How about it?"

"A race Mr Brogan? How will your male ego cope with being beaten by a bunch of women?" asked Cassie, smiling sweetly at Ben.

"Oh, I don't know? Same as a strong willed child like you getting beaten by a bunch of kids, I reckon!"

The rudder was installed on Saturday and pronounced leak free when the tide came in to refloat Serendipity. Ben and Cassie pulled her back into deeper water, back next to Ben's boat, where she had first arrived – back where she sat after smashing into Ben's pride and joy. He was able to laugh about it now and tomorrow he would find out just how good a sailor Cassie was. He knew she was good – nobody sails across the Pacific on their own without good skills and confidence. *The confidence of a strong willed child*, Ben chuckled to himself as they tied the yacht securely to the wharf.

After lunch on Sunday, Ben and Cassie took off their sail covers in readiness for the big race. They had been secretly eyeing each other, but generally laughing a lot as they prepared their boats. The two car loads of crew arrived almost at the same time and soon the wharf was full of happy smiling Yolngu faces. Cassie and Ben organised their crew and prepared to cast off.

The Granites is a small rocky island in the middle of Gove Harbour. Local white miners and their families often used it for picnics and barbeques and the handful of racing sailors at the yacht club, would use the island as a marker on most racing days.

As they were about to leave, Ben walked over to Serendipity and finalised the rules with Cassie.

"Right then, we'll motor out to the point at North Beach, raise the sails and when we're nose to nose, you say go."

"Suits me Ben. May the best man win!" They shook hands before Cassie turned and jumped aboard, her ponytail bouncing in the light breeze.

Ben and Cassie both shared the freedom and love that the salt water and fresh breezes had to offer. They also looked forward to the excitement of not only sailing their beloved boats after a long lay-off, but the excitement of matching their wits and skills against someone they felt close to, tied to, in a way that both man and woman become tied in both body and soul.

Cassie installed Rose on the tiller. Rose was shocked, at first reluctant, but with Cassie encouraging her, soon began to enjoy the experience. Karen was then shown the rudiments of operating the jib winch sheets, before Cassie leapt gracefully up to the mast and raised the mainsail. In the same way, Ben had Garrawarra and his wife trained as instant sailors and as they approached the cliffs below the meeting place at North beach, both boats had sails raised and engines turned off. Cassie and Ben had made contact on radio and as the boats rounded the point side by side, Cassie shouted go and set about trimming the sails and giving orders to Rose about which direction to steer.

The race took about three hours, neither boat getting any real advantage as they crossed over in a tacking duel, one time Ben in front, the next time Cassie. At the helm, Rose and Garrawarra enjoyed being on the sea, the wind providing a tranquillity they rarely found on land. The young boys sitting at the bow pointed excitedly at a pod of dolphins that appeared from nowhere and began to leap out of the water, surfing the bow waves.

"Missed me that time Kookaburra!" yelled Ben as Cassie crossed immediately behind his stern.

"I can hit you any time I like – better watch out next time!" Cassie was elated as she breathed in the fresh salt air of the south east trades. Serendipity was such a sweet boat to sail and old as she was; Cassie was determined to beat Ben in his new sleek machine. She started to yearn for the open waters again, imagining what it would be like to sail out of Gove harbour with Ben at her side and head out to exotic ports in Bali or Borneo. She could see Ben was a good sailor; he was constantly tuning his sails and supporting Garrawarra on the helm.

The island was beautiful; a giant rain tree perched behind white sands dotted with giant grey boulders. They were careful to weave round the submerged rocks, Cassie following right behind Ben, assuming he had local knowledge. They scooted back towards the point, Ben still in front and Cassie frantically trying to squeeze every ounce of wind into her sails as they neared the finish line. With only one hundred yards to go, she saw Ben's jib sail go loose and start flapping madly in the wind. His boat slowed rapidly. Cassie took the opportunity to pass Ben and cut off the wind to his sails momentarily, slowing his forward progress even more. She was elated. The all-girl crew squealed with pleasure, as they looked around to see Ben's boat back on the move again. They waved and began jumping excitedly, as if they had just won the Sydney to Hobart yacht race.

11 Garma Festival

The sun was another ball of orange resting on the rim of the ocean as Ben and Cassie lounged in Serendipity's cockpit, plastic champagne glasses in hand.

"I think a toast is in order. Much as it pains me to accept defeat by – a girl. To the winner of the inaugural Umbakala Cup – Miss Cassie Greenway!" Ben put his glass down and clapped furiously before adding, "Speech, speech – the crowd wants to know how you did it. What exactly is Miss Greenway's secret to success?

"Aw, shucks, 'twarn't nuthin'. Secret? That's easy, the secret is to smash your opponent's boat well before the race, then offer to fix it and hide lead in the repair! So that's your answer Mr Brogan. Cheat!"

"Really, Miss Greenway? I would never have taken such a sweet little Californian gal as a cheat – perhaps she was just a teeny weeny bit lucky we lost our jib sheet right at the end of the race?"

"Oh really Mr Brogan? Perhaps it's just that American gals are better sailors than Aussie boys?"

"Oh really Miss Greenway?" Ben retorted as he lunged one handed at Cassie's waist, tickling her underarms till she was giggling uncontrollably, spilling large drops of champagne over her leg.

"Hey, don't waste that, it's Chateau Umbakala, all of two months old!" As he spoke Ben leaned over and pressed his lips to the champagne on Cassie's thigh, lapping with pleasure. Cassie stopped giggling and sighed, bubbles of delight frothing over her body, before Ben suddenly stopped, as if trying to control himself, to stop what came to happen so naturally between them. In the pause, Cassie seized her moment, put down her near empty glass, grabbed Ben's leg and lifted it onto her lap, then grasped his calf in a bear hug. She began to tickle the soles of his feet, looking over her shoulder for a reaction. Ben was giggling and laughing in a frenzy.

"Oh – no – ha, ha – stop – no, stop, stop ..." pleaded Ben as he thrashed about.

"Give in?"

"Yes – yes!"

"Who's the winner?"

"You are – you are! Cassie – stop, stop!"

Ben took deep breaths, a huge smile on his face as he regained his composure.

"Hey, you fight dirty. How did you know that was my Achilles heel; that I was so ticklish on my feet?"

"Oh, didn't I tell you? Didn't I tell you I was tickle wrestling champion at college?"

"You sure know how to hurt a guy Cassie – first you beat me at arm wrestling, then Scrabble, then yacht racing and now tickle wrestling? I'm beginning to wonder if there's anything I can beat you at?"

"Probably nothing, but I don't mind if you keep on trying – maybe one day?" Cassie smiled as she poured out the last of the champagne. The sun had disappeared, leaving a tinge of bright colours in the sky. She wanted to sit here all night with this man, just to play and chat and feel safe – feel loved. But tomorrow they would head off to Garma. Ben was to help set up the stall with Rose and the other women. This perfect day had to end early, Ben would understand, he seemed after all to be the perfect gentleman, yet was possessed with a boyish spirit of fun; just like her father.

Next morning, Ben loaded the trestle tables onto his truck while Cassie carried out the well packed art works for the Garma display. She tossed her rucksack into the back of the truck, packed with clothes and essentials for camping out for a week. She was excited, as she carefully loaded the boxes, treating each one like a valuable treasure. Ben covered the load with a tarpaulin and was tying it down, when he saw Karen walking down toward the art centre. With her was a tall athletic looking Yolngu man – like all Yolngu, he had skinny calves and ankles, but this man had a powerful chest and strong wiry arms. It was Simon Gamalka; one of Ben's building workers, also Garrawarra's cousin. Ben had arranged for Gamalka to be Karen's minder while the others were at the Garma festival. He was a good worker but he could be spared for one week – just in case.

"Namirri Gamalka. You know Cassie of course?"

"Namirri Cassie. You go Garma, first time?"

"Yes Gamalka, I'm really excited about going. Thanks for staying to help Karen while I'm gone; I'm sure the building team will miss you." Karen looked across to Gamalka, beaming. The look registered with Cassie. It looked as if Karen had her sights set on a new man. Was it possible for a half aboriginal from another area to be with a Yolngu man from Arnhem Land? She hoped so; it was time that Karen found happiness. Cassie jumped into the truck next to Ben, before they drove down the road toward Garma.

Clouds of orange dust behind the truck had begun to settle, as they slowly bumped over the grassy field. They passed the take-away food huts where operators were busy setting up for the day. There were white troopys parked under every tree and groups of people, black and white were already milling in all directions. As with every other day, it was hot, but the steadfast trade wind brought a welcome relief as it blew through the branches onto the high plateau, and cooling ever so slightly the field in the middle of nowhere.

The truck edged past a sea of blue and green tents, set up in anticipation of tourists, performers and artists. At last, in front of them they found the canvas and steel stalls, assembled for the exhibitions and they wasted no time finding the one reserved for Umbakala art. Parking next to the stall, they unloaded the boxes onto the grass, and then Ben set up the trestle tables. They were a team again, working and sweating side by side till it was all done. Cassie stepped back to admire their handiwork, when the first visitors arrived; a young couple with back-packs, chatting in what sounded like German.

"Will you be okay now Cassie? I have to get back to town now; we've made a good start on building that second house."

"I'll be fine thanks Ben. Rose and the girls should be here soon, so I'll be able to find my tent and be completely organised."

Ben grinned and winked at Cassie, before giving her a hug. A reluctant goodbye. He wanted desperately to stay with her, to enjoy the colour and drama of all that Garma had to offer. As he held her briefly in his arms, he felt that familiar feeling of joy and comfortable warmth that now only came into his life when he was with Cassie.

"Anyway, I'll be back on Friday, I'm keen to see the finals of the dance competition. It'll be good to cheer on the Umbakala mob. I'll also try and track down Mike and see what he has to say about those money matters – last I heard he was still supposed to be in Darwin."

"I'd almost forgotten about him. Remember, we're having dinner here on Friday night, then there's the evening entertainment in the outdoor stage area – you will stay won't you?" Cassie looked up at Ben, her eyes showing some vulnerability, a soft feminine gaze, still uncertain of Ben and his feelings for her. It took all of Ben's willpower to walk away from this woman – this beguiling creature with the azure eyes and angelic face.

Ben drove slowly back toward Umbakala on the winding dirt roads, smiling and singing softly to himself as he daydreamed. Already missing her, Ben suddenly realised how content he was, now that Cassie and he had sorted out their differences. Now it felt that they were on common ground, a united front. Before Cassie had come, he would have used such times to think about his work, the materials he had to order, the building tasks for the day, the people he had to talk to. Now, all he saw in his mind were pictures of Cassie; pictures of Cassie when she first arrived, when he saw her disoriented with a bloody nose; pictures of Cassie arriving at the building site for the first time; pictures of Cassie showing him the art centre damage, and – that kiss; Cassie barbequing fish on her boat; Cassie in church; pictures of Cassie naked through the porthole of Serendipity; Cassie repairing his boat; pictures of arm wrestling, tickling, drinking champagne in sunset evenings and that boat race. Ben ran and re-ran the mental movie reels feeling both serene and excited. When he was with her, he could hardly tear his eyes away, watching her curves, her graceful movements, her lissom walk. Now, they were apart, he was unable to take his mind off her. He had never thought he would feel like this again. Friday could not come soon enough for Ben and so it was just as well that he would have plenty of work to keep him busy, even if he had a depleted building team because of Garma and the dance festival.

Each day at lunch time Ben visited the art centre to make sure Karen was okay. He could see that Karen and Gamalka had already broken cultural barriers. It was just as well it seemed to be a quiet week because Ben was not sure how much work was getting done. He always seemed to interrupt them giggling and they seemed keen to reassure him that he was not needed, almost shooing him out the door. Ben was glad Karen no longer had him in her sights. She was a beautiful and alluring woman, but no match for Cassie, no match for the woman who now held him captivated by her charms, captivated and in her thrall.

Every day, Ben also popped into the council offices looking for Mike, eager to see what Mike would have to say for himself against the evidence of embezzlement and dishonesty. Each day he spoke to Lesley, who told him that Mike had been in the office briefly on Tuesday morning, then told her he had to go back to Darwin again. Ben contemplated what his absence meant. Mike had missed their appointed meeting – what was he up to? Was his absence in any way linked to Dumatja? No matter, he would be held accountable one day; perhaps his leaving might solve one of the problems the Umbakala community faced. Yet the hardest problem of all was Dumatja. Was he gone for good? What would happen if he returned? What if he appeared at Garma? Would the clan leaders somehow be able to deal with him, to punish him?

When Ben caught up with Garrawarra, he discovered that his friend had made it his business to find out if Dumatja had returned or if there was any news of his whereabouts. In previous years, Dumatja had been one of the lead dancers at Garma as a senior man with much of the knowledge of Yolngu song and dance. He was now nowhere to be found, even some of his clan were concerned, not concerned for his physical wellbeing as they knew he could find bush tucker and hunt to live off the land,. They too were concerned about his mental state, for his recent extreme behaviour.

On Friday, Ben had arranged to finish work mid-afternoon. He had packed his swag and a picnic blanket and was looking forward to lying under the stars during the evening concert with Cassie. Maybe, if it felt right, he would camp a night or two before helping Cassie pack up the display. He drove much quicker this time, keen to see the entire ceremonial dance held in the late afternoon. The fourteen communities who were there would dance one after the other to show off their skills, their different stories, to each other and to visitors who came from all over the world. As his truck crept into the Garma arena, past grassy car parks full of white four wheel drives, he could feel his heart beating faster, as he heard the beating of Yolngu clap sticks, excited at the ancient mystical culture he was about to embrace, excited at the beautiful woman he might also embrace.

As soon as he switched off the engine, Ben grabbed his gear and marched straight toward Cassie's stall. His schoolboy eagerness was soon overtaken by manly yearnings when he saw her petite figure standing in the shade of the canvas, talking with a group of tourists. He stopped and stared from a distance, watching the sun gleam in her hair as she stepped outside for a moment, the breeze pressing her fine skirt against the curves of her legs as she stood at the entrance making parting gestures and words with visitors.

"Hello Kookaburra, I'm back!" declared Ben as he grasped her playfully from behind.

"Oh, you frightened me!" Cassie turned while Ben still had his hands attached to her waist, looking down at her with the warmest smile. She stood on her toes and planted a kiss on Ben's cheek, at the same time that her hands were pushing down on his forearms, releasing his eager hold.

"Not now, Buffalo Ben – this gal still has work to do. Give me a few minutes and we'll close up the stall. The dancing is about to start."

"How was the stall; was it worth the effort?"

"Oh Ben, it's been fantastic! We've made so many sales and the potential internet deals we're going to do, is way beyond what I had hoped for!"

Ben grinned at her enthusiasm. That was one of the things he loved to see in her.

"That's great. Hey, can I park my swag here? We can take the picnic rug to sit on the grass and watch the ceremony."

Before long Ben and Cassie were walking hand-in-hand toward the central clearing, which was already surrounded by people sitting on rugs and chairs and many more standing close to the singers and didgeridoo players who were settled under a makeshift corrugated steel shelter. The buzz of excitement from the crowd electrified Ben and Cassie as they chose a spot some distance from where a tall Yolngu man stood with a microphone in front of the musicians. He was dressed in western clothes and was wearing a white cowboy hat, the shade of which did not appear to darken his face. The crowd hushed with anticipation as the man spoke. It was a welcome speech in almost perfect English, an introduction to the musicians and dance in both English and Yolngu; it was an explanation of the symbolism of Garma and their endeavour to take the ancient Yolngu culture to the rest of the world.

They sat quietly in the warmth of the afternoon and the glow of the colourful crowd. Blue eyes locked in brown eyes, hand resting in hand, waiting for the first dancers to come into the arena. Cassie felt her spirit soaring to new heights. She had for that moment forgotten her reservations about Ben and the uncertainty of how he felt about her. She had forgotten her past life and the bustle of the rest of the world as the drone and hum of the didgeridoos energised the crowd. They were soon accompanied by the nasal dirge of the male singers and sharp clicking of the clap sticks. A group of Yolngu dancers emerged from the nearby gum trees, led by the men and boys, women and girls at the rear. Their black skin was painted with white ochre tribal markings. Some wore brightly coloured headbands tied firmly against wiry black hair. They saw the bright blue lap laps and bare legs stomping in the dusty grass to the mystical tune of the sounds that hovered around them. Neither Cassie nor Ben understood the sudden head movements, gestures emulating animals like kangaroos or emus, gestures talking to the long lost spirits of warriors who had gone before them, but they were transfixed by the atmosphere. Still holding hands, they were absorbed in the ancient song and dance of first one tribe, then another, then another. Between dances, Cassie would smile at Ben as they listened to the Yolngu announcer in the cowboy hat give an explanation of who was dancing and what the dancers were trying to say. The moment was perfect; a perfection that neither wanted to end. The spectacle of senses they knew was unique in Australia and in the rest of the world. They each felt the privilege of witnessing the ancient art, the history, the culture in a land that was slowly dying.

The sun had crept below the tops of the gum trees that surrounded the Garma arena when the last of the dancers left the earth stage. Cassie and Ben gathered up their rug and set about finding Rose, Sarah and Emily. They had agreed to have dinner together in the outdoor mess hall, before setting back into the outdoor arena to savour the sounds of the evening's entertainment of music and dance which would be of a more contemporary flavour.

Ben felt a bit of an outsider as he sat with the women at the sturdy outdoor picnic tables. While eating the plain but bountiful meals, they were chatting excitedly about their week of connecting with people they had never met before, from places they had never heard of, to people from distant clans, all somehow related in the Yolngu ancestry web. He watched and observed how naturally Cassie related to these women from such a diverse culture. Her warmth and kindness flowed like a light rain on a parched land and Ben sat watching proudly, with an ever building sense of affection, as Cassie sat beside him.

It was dark by the time their group had finished eating and they could hear the distant twang of electric guitars warming up the giant amplifiers. The stage was a tall earth mound at the opposite end of the clearing from where the dancing had been held. Behind it was a large permanent screen, like in drive-in movies; a projection hut some distance away. As Ben and Cassie walked across the darkened field, they could see a group of Yolngu teenage boys with guitars and drum sets on the stage. Scattered over an area the size of a football field, were shadowy figures of people, both Yolngu and visitors, some sitting or lying on the ground, some sitting on folding chairs, others standing or milling. They found a private spot near the edge of the field away from the crowds. The stage was still easily seen and the powerful amplifiers would ensure no sounds would go unnoticed. Ben laid out the rug and the two pillows he had brought in the truck. Cassie was pleased by his thoughtfulness; it had been a long hard week on her feet. Relaxing here under the stars, a pillow under her head, beside her a beautiful man, was stuff dreams were made of, she decided as she lay down and breathed out a very audible sigh.

"Ooh Ben, this is just perfect. Have you ever seen such a black sky and bright stars?"
Ben lay down next to Cassie and reached out for her hand. He slowly pulled her fingers up to his mouth and kissed her hand. A chivalrous knight.

"I've seen a few, but I don't think the stars have been so bright, not for a long time anyway."

They lay quietly side by side, languid, content, at peace with each other and with the world, when the first notes of Yolngu rock music reached their ears. They were pleased to be far enough away to be able to talk comfortably, yet still hear the music of the young band. A group of aboriginal girls were introduced next - a contemporary dance group from Darwin. Ben and Cassie watched appreciatively as the dancers interpreted ancient Yolngu dance with modern jazz ballet movements.

The night continued with different Yolngu bands from Arnhem Land communities, taking turns to entertain. Ben had asked Cassie about life in San Francisco and she had all but filled in the missing gaps of her life story, finishing with her life with James. While Cassie talked, head propped on a pillow, Ben lay on his side, one hand propping his head, their faces an intimate breath away. Cassie felt a surge of pleasure rush through her body as Ben brushed a hand over her belly and reached for her hand, linking fingers. Her heart began to race madly as Ben slowly blocked out some of the stars, his lips coming nearer and nearer. She was silent, her mouth open and willing, then finally she felt the softness of his lips on hers, gentle and caressing. This was completely unlike that first kiss. This was tenderness and love and a promise of passion to come. Cassie put her arms around Ben's neck and gladly drew him closer as their lips separated and each felt the pleasure of the perfect kiss; tongues and lips melded in the magic of this moment – the moment they had hoped for, but neither expected. Neither had dreamed of such bliss as the sound of a Yolngu love song washed over them, the cooling breeze brushed their skin in a caress and the light of a thousand stars lit up their faces with a midnight glow.

They stayed locked in the endless moment of this kiss, embracing, touching. Ben's free hand had stroked the nape of Cassie's neck, and had slipped under her light blouse, lightly tracing the journey of his intent on her warm back but he held back from more intimate touching. He lost himself in the beauty and passion, yet somehow maintained the boundaries he felt Cassie wanted, deserved.

"Ben, I'm not sure." Cassie groaned in a hoarse whisper, when they eventually surfaced for air.

"Not sure of what Cassie? Not sure of me?"

"Not sure of my mind; everything in my heart feels so right. Ben, I've dreamed of feeling – feeling like this for what seems like my whole life. I know you feel it too Ben – but – I don't quite know how to say this."

Ben leaned down and kissed Cassie on the lips again, wanting more, but curbing his desire as he spoke.

"Kookaburra, you can tell me anything. I think we should be totally honest with each other."

"It's just that – just that you once said you were sort of married and sort of not. You've mentioned Laura but haven't told me anything about her. I mean, if you still love Laura and hope for a reconciliation, then we can't do this. To be fair to each other, we have to go our own ways. Maybe with this Dumatja thing, I'll just have to leave Umbakala and that would solve our problem – your problem. Does any of that make sense?" The dagger of pain twisted in Cassie's gut as she thought of leaving him.

"You're right Cassie; I have to tell you everything. You see I still love Laura; I think I'll always love her – but."

"But what Ben? You can't love two women, be with two women – you know that's not right." A sense of relief came over Cassie that at last she had been able to challenge Ben. Perhaps now she would discover the truth?

"Let me start from the beginning. After Laura and I were married five years ago, we decided to live on our yacht and sail north from Sydney and see if we liked it. If it felt right, we were just going to keep going, sail around the world. You see, she was a good sailor, grew up with boats in the family, just like you."

"So what happened?"

"Well, we got as far as Brisbane and decided to work for six months to save money to keep going. So that was good, we lived on the boat at the marina; I worked for a builder and Laura found accounting temp work. Laura hated accounting, but it paid the bills. Anyway, one night we were sitting in the cockpit and while I was having a glass of wine, Laura said she didn't want any. That surprised me because we always had a glass after dinner." Ben paused to see if Cassie was still attentive.

"Go on Ben, what then?"

"Well, what she told me nearly blew my socks off. She said we were going to have a baby."

"Weren't you happy Ben? Didn't you want to have children?" Cassie was surprised; she had seen him play with Garrawarra's boys.

"No, it's not that, it's just that we'd spent nearly two years planning this sailing adventure. I thought that would be it and we'd have to sell the boat, buy a house in suburbia and do all those things normal people do. I-I just wasn't ready for it, that's all." Ben paused and lay down on his back, crossing his hands over his chest. As he moved away, Cassie saw the nightlights reflecting moisture in his eyes. She sensed Ben's pain and wanted to comfort him, but still wanted to know what happened to cause his pain, to make him run away, like so many people up here – perhaps like herself. Cassie put an arm over Ben and snuggled into him. She wanted him to know he was not alone.

"So what happened Ben? Did you leave her? You wouldn't have abandoned her; she was pregnant." Cassie fought not to feel disappointment as she waited for Ben's reply.

"No – we had a fight. I mean, not really a fight, we never fought. Oh, we had disagreements, but somehow we always managed to find compromise. But this? This would spoil all our plans and abortion was out of the question. Neither of us wanted that. Anyway, Laura told me that she had an appointment for an ultrasound the next day and she was going with Sandy."

"Who's Sandy?"

"Her sister. She lives in Brisbane. Anyway, we kind of went to bed not talking to each other. We'd never done that." Ben's voice quavered as he spoke. Cassie leaned over and kissed him lightly on the cheek.

"Go on Ben, what happened next?"

"Well – the next morning, nothing changed, only I offered to go with her. After all, it was our baby and I felt I should go, but she said, 'No, no, I've already made arrangements with Sandy.' Then she just got in a cab and left."

"What do you mean left? She left you?"

Ben rolled over onto his side facing Cassie; tears streaming down his face as Cassie gently stroked his back, starting to well up herself. He paused to compose himself before he allowed himself to continue.

"I never saw her again Cassie." He started to sob as soon as the words were out. Cassie embraced Ben, kissing his tears and then on the lips – a gentle butterfly, just to comfort, to let him know he was loved, without words needing to be spoken.

When he had calmed his tears and quietened his sobs, Cassie spoke while gently rubbing Ben's brow.

"Something happened to her, didn't it Ben?"

"Y-yes. She, she was in a car accident – traffic lights – there was this van – hit her side on. She died on the way to hospital. I didn't know. I rang her after she left to tell her it was okay; to tell her that I wanted to have this baby. You see, I saw a yacht on our marina and it had netting and safety lines; all set up for their baby. I saw them that morning with their little baby crawling around the deck they looked so happy! Cassie, I wanted to tell her, but her phone was off. I kept calling until finally Sandy answered." He started sobbing again, face screwed up in pain, but quieter this time.

"Oh Ben, I didn't know. I don't know how you could cope with such tragedy - and the baby."

"I'd already started to imagine our life. We'd have a girl just like Laura and then a tough determined little boy. We'd take them surfing and sailing. And now? This, this was unimaginable and it was all my fault."

"No it wasn't. Ben, it was an accident."

"Cassie, if I had not been so selfish and just been happy when Laura first told me, it would have been *me* driving her to the hospital – the accident wouldn't have happened. Laura and the baby would be alive today." Ben closed his eyes as he lay on his side facing Cassie. Entwined in their embrace, Cassie looked across at the moonlight shadows dancing on Ben's sharp cheekbones. In the background was the noise of cicadas and frogs; the concert had finished and most of the people had already left the arena. As she watched Ben, tears rolled slowly across her cheeks and she knew. She knew she could never leave this man. She snuggled closer into the shelter of his strong arms and legs and fell asleep.

12 Crocodile Creek

Cassie woke the following morning to the sound of chirping birds and the dull ache of a sore shoulder. She was startled when opening her eyes, all she could see were two warm latte eyes smiling down at her.

"Good morning Kookaburra. Did you sleep alright?"

"Like a log, but I'm a bit stiff like a log as well. I don't think we changed position all night!" Cassie smiled as she looked across and disentangled her legs from Ben's.

"I've been watching you sleeping for about half an hour. You never moved – I thought I might have to give you mouth to mouth to wake you up!"

"Oh Ben, I think we did enough resuscitating last night," laughed Cassie as she pushed Ben in the chest and rolled over before slowly standing and stretching like a tiger cat.

"Come on Buffalo Ben. Let's grab some breakfast so I can set up the stall for the last day."

They moved on to the dining camp, talking and laughing like two best friends. Cassie felt a sense of relief after hearing Ben's heartbreaking story the night before and was glad that Ben was himself again this morning, not maudlin as he had been last night. She guessed that Ben had never told his tragic tale to anyone before and she felt honoured that he had shared his pain with her. Yet, Cassie still felt a nagging uncertainty. After all, Ben had told her that that he still loved Laura. Perhaps it was all too soon for him. But what about her? How long would she be willing to wait and would he want her to?

After breakfast, Cassie opened the display stall for the final time with Rose and the girls. The girls had seemed delighted to see Cassie and Ben walking toward them holding hands. Cassie had seen the hidden whispers behind dark hands and heard the giggles. She glanced to see if Ben had noticed but he seemed oblivious or maybe he did not care.

The blue sky days in the tropical dry season were nearly always predictable. People would reach for hats and shade as the sun heated the still, warm land. Ben sat in the dappled shade of a Casuarina tree near the art centre stall, sometimes chatting to visitors from overseas, sometimes with a Yolngu friend, but mostly with Cassie. Theirs seemed now to be a never ending conversation as they explored new topics as if they were climbing new mountains or sailing new oceans. It was one of those days that raced along swiftly and when night came, it was as if it had never existed. Cassie felt a new raw energy, as they strolled hand in hand from the outdoor mess hall toward the raised earth stage where a new crop of musicians was setting up for the evening.

"Yothu Yindi are playing tonight Cassie. I thought you might like to get up and dance with me, you know, burn off some of that energy I know you've got."

"You bet, only I don't know how to do any Yolngu dancing."

"Don't worry, it's just modern stuff, but then, I'd like to do some of that old fashioned stuff with you..."

"Old fashioned stuff?"

"Yeah, that's right – that's where the man gets to actually hold the woman!" As he said the words, Ben put a hand round Cassie's waist and took her hand with the other. Before they knew it, they were moving their feet in a waltz-like embrace in the middle of the field, in the middle of nowhere, dancing to a tune in their heads; dancing like there was no one else in the world, under the stars, like two lovers who knew the intimacy of each other's movements.

It was only the band striking up their first number that spoiled the enchantment and drew them back to the crowds of people and the undercurrent of energy in front of the stage. Ben and Cassie joined in with the Yolngu and white dancers swaying to the meld of ancient and new guitar chords and drum beats. Cassie lost herself in the power of this passionate music, then lost herself in the powerful arms of Ben as they slow danced the last dance, before heading back to Cassie's tent, where again they slept soundly, snuggled up in each other's arms and living for the moment, absorbing themselves in the now, for the now was too precious, too good to worry about what tomorrow might bring.

Cassie thought that even the coffee tasted better that morning, as she sat opposite Ben at breakfast. She looked at his slightly crooked nose and sharp cheek bones and marvelled at how he grew more handsome each day. She remembered how Mario had once seemed more handsome to her on that first day when she met them both. Now, as she looked closely at Ben's lips, memorising every shape and curve of his face, she could see his inner beauty, his energy and passion, right there in his eyes and all over his beautiful face. She leant forward and with the tip of her tongue kissed the tiny pale scar above his left eyebrow. She was annoyed when her daydream of Ben evaporated with the sound of her mobile phone ringing.

"Hello, Cassie here."

"Yes Karen." Cassie stood and listened carefully – the line was not clear. "Buyers from New York want to talk to me?" "I suppose I'll have to. I'll try to be there in an hour – okay, see you soon."

Ben leaned across toward Cassie and enveloped both of her hands in the security of his own.

"You're not flying off are you Kookaburra?"

"I'm afraid I have to. It seems those Americans are keen to talk to *me*. Apparently Djingala, that's Mike's receptionist, called Karen and said that they had to leave on a flight at midday."

"Can't Karen deal with them?"

"Guess not; they asked especially to see me. Suggestion is they have a lot of money to spend."

"Wonder why they didn't come to Garma?"

"I guess they didn't have time. Doesn't sound like I've got much choice," sighed Cassie.

"What about packing up your art stall?"

"Would you mind Ben? Helping Rose and the girls? I'll meet you at the art centre later this morning. Hey - just had an idea. Maybe we could go for a sail this afternoon?"

"Hmm, maybe I'll let you take the helm of my boat? Of course, only if there are no other boats in the vicinity."

"You rat, Ben Brogan!" Cassie tousled Ben's hair, as she sat down on his lap. The parting kiss that followed now seemed the most natural thing to both of them as Cassie wrapped her arms around Ben's neck and once again felt the love of this man radiating from his lips. She was now waiting for him to tell her he loved her. She knew he loved her, but this is the way it had to be – the man had to say it first. Cassie wanted to hear the words from Ben, not just feel his love. Maybe he would tell her when they were sailing? Perhaps he was like James and would never say the words?

Cassie felt a twinge of sadness as she drove past the Garma arena toward the exit road. She had never felt so alive as in the last few days in this place of exotic music and dance, with the man she adored. She felt gloomy as she pondered the uncertainty of her future here - a boss who did not like her and was stealing money and a cultural leader who wanted her gone and was going to do everything in his power to make sure that she never returned. Cassie had always been a planner, a decision maker, someone who knew what she wanted and where she was going, except where James was concerned. Now she was filled with uncertainty. She wanted to stay, but how could she? She wanted to be with Ben, but how would that be possible? After all, he said himself he would stay and finish training the Yolngu building team. And what about Laura? Could Ben love her as much as he had loved Laura? Cassie's mind went round in circles without hope of a solution.

Cassie arrived at the art centre hoping the American buyers were still around. Parked out the front was a battered and dust covered troopy she did not recognise, but assumed it had belonged to Simon Gamalka, Karen's Yolngu minder. The front door was open as she stepped inside to the cool hum of the air conditioning.

"Karen, are you there?" Cassie called out. There was no answer. Cassie hesitated for a moment, puzzled, then peered into the main gallery. The display lights were turned off and the gallery was in semi-darkness, with only the one small high window providing light. *That's unusual. We always have the light on. Maybe there's a power-cut?* She flicked the switch, lighting up the gallery, before walking round the corner of the freshly painted wall. Cassie was pleased to see that Karen had hung new artworks, aesthetically arranged by colour and shape.

"Karen – where are you? Gamalka, are you there?" A fist formed in her stomach as the silence continued, shattered only by the pad of her own sandalled footsteps as she walked toward the light switch of the second gallery. She turned suddenly, when she heard a click from the direction of Karen's work room and the store room. This time she raised her voice even louder, the quiver in her words betraying her anxiety.

"Hello – is, is anyone there?" She stepped into Karen's room. A cup of coffee sat on the desk, still steaming and a half eaten piece of toast and jam lay on the plate next to it. Cassie gulped, her anxiety tight in her throat. She could see the darkness of the store room through the gap of the partly opened door. *Where could she be? I hope she's okay.* Cassie began to worry that Karen might have had some sort of accident as she pushed the door of the store room. It opened with a loud creak. Cassie crept slowly inside, flipping the light switch as she entered. Karen was sitting on a chair, her hands tied up with packing tape. Her mouth sealed with tape. Cassie gasped in horror, clutching her hands to her open mouth. Suddenly the door slammed shut and from behind the door, Cassie caught the glint of shiny metal out of the corner of her eye. Her mouth went dry, pulse racing, she turned just as Dumatja spoke.

"You turn now Miss Cassie. I tell you leave. Why you not leave when I tell you leave? AH?"

Cassie backed away from the menacing eyes which seemed to pierce her soul – those sharp eyes which seemed more dangerous than the long steel blade he was pointing in her direction. She froze, unable to speak, remembering Alanja's words, his advice not to be alone.

"Hold out hands – NOW!" Dumatja grabbed a roll of tape twisting and wrapping it round Cassie's wrists. She could smell the stale stench of his unwashed shirt, the putrid breath of tobacco smoke mixed with marijuana. After he had taped her mouth, his fingers dug into her forearm and he led her roughly out of the storeroom, closing the door quietly behind them. Even in the cool air of the gallery, Cassie was sweating freely, the palms of her hands cold and clammy, the cramping in her stomach now almost unbearable as she gasped for breath. Her mind froze at the thought of what this evil man might do to her. Dumatja opened the front door of the art centre and peered out. Seeing that no one was about, he pushed Cassie outside toward the battered troopy. He shovelled her into the passenger side, forcing her to crouch on the floor, ramming her face onto the seat. She almost retched at the stink of urine and blood in the seat. She turned her head towards Dumatja, now in the driver's seat.

Only Rose remained to help Ben pack up the art displays; the other women were busy having a reunion with relatives from another community. Ben could see from her face that Rose looked troubled and assumed she was still sad from the death of her mother, even though the funeral rites were now completed. While they were still packing, Rose paused for a minute, then looked at Ben.

"Ben – you know we love Miss Cassie? She care about us – she care about our painting. I know how she feel about you Ben. She very good woman Ben - What you going to do about that? I no want see Cassie hurt."

Ben was taken aback by Rose's forthright statement. She always seemed so quiet and he knew that she must care for Cassie a great deal. She had spoken with heartfelt sincerity. He felt like it had been Cassie's father asking him if his intentions were honourable, yet he had not even told Cassie that he loved her.

"Rose, I don't know what to say. I would never want to hurt Cassie – I , I, have feelings for her ..."

"Then you marry her Ben. You marry her or you walk away." Rose immediately resumed packing with that pronouncement, leaving no room for further discussion. Ben suddenly felt sick in his stomach as he kept working. He thought about how he had let down Laura, about how his love had failed her. He was afraid if he gave his all to Cassie, it would not be good enough. He was afraid his love would not be sufficient to protect her, to keep her safe.

Rose sat silently in the passenger seat of the truck, as they drove back to Umbakala. Ben was looking forward to sailing with Cassie that afternoon. He chuckled to himself when he imagined their conversation about which boat to sail. To Ben it did not matter, it would be a joy to be on the water with Cassie, just like it was with Laura. But what then? Could he tell her he loved her? Was it too soon to give his heart and his life to this beautiful woman?

Ben's spirits rose when he saw Cassie's troopy parked in front of the art centre. He stopped the truck next to it and jumped out, eager to see Cassie. He quickly opened the truck door for Rose. Ben was surprised to find the front door unlocked. He opened it and followed Rose inside, calling out to Cassie as they looked around the art centre.

"Strange, Rose, she's not in her office or the galleries?"

"I have bad feeling Ben. Something bad happen here." She moved toward the store room door, beckoning Ben to come. Then they heard a muffled cry. Thinking it was Cassie, they burst into the room where Karen sat; gagged and bound to a chair. Within seconds they had removed the tape from Karen's mouth.

"Oh, oh, thank God you're here Ben. It's – it's Dumatja; he's got her. He's got Cassie!" Karen was almost shrieking, somewhere between hysteria and sobs as she fought to catch her breath. Rose put her large arms around Karen, remembering the last time Dumatja had caused this woman pain.

"Karen, you have to tell me. Where did he take her? Is she okay?" Shouted Ben, agitated, concerned, his brow furrowed. He knew that he had to act quickly. He could not even let himself think that he might be too late.

"I – I don't know Ben. He just tied her up – that's all I know," wailed Karen in between sobs.

"Ben – find Alanja or Bulangi, tell them what happen – they know what to do," said Rose in a loud whisper. Ben turned and sprinted to his truck, there was no time to lose. The spinning tyres lifted a cloud of dust as he powered the truck out of the car park and onto the road toward the council building. He decided to drive to Alanja's place first, then the church; he might still be at the service. As the council building appeared before him, Ben was surprised to recognise Alanja's troopy parked out front. He skidded the wheels in the dirt and did not even shut the truck door as he raced up to the front door. It was open. He burst through, calling out to his friend.

"Alanja – are you there?"

"Yo – Ben – we in meeting room."

A familiar sight. Alanja and Bulangi were standing by the window smoking; in earnest discussion.

"Thank God you're here – listen, we've got an emergency, Dumatja's taken Cassie from the art centre! We've got to find her!"

The two Yolngu elders looked at each other, then at Ben, before asking Ben for the full story.

"Hmm, we think we have big problem with CEO; that not so important now."

"What do you mean?" asked Ben, a puzzled expression on his face.

"Mike phone me, say he gone – say he leave Umbakala for good. Not say why."

"Because he's been stealing money, that's why." Ben hissed through his teeth, not even caring how angry he sounded. "Look, you must have some idea? Where would he have taken Cassie?"

Alanja rubbed his chin. Ben could see both men were deep in thought

"Nothing like this ever happen before Ben. You say he have knife and tie her up? This not Yolngu way?" Alanja turned hopefully toward Bulangi with raised eyebrows. "We could ask Dumatja family? Dumatja father?"

Ben ran his fingers through his hair, pacing back and forth. Then suddenly he stopped and turned, before punching an open palm with his fist.

"That's it! Remember what he did to Karen? I think it was that creek where the croc lives - I've been to the beach for a barbeque – quick we have to go there!"

Again, Alanja and Bulangi looked at each other before Alanja spoke slowly.

"Yo, yo – that sacred place, dreaming place. Dumatja do special ceremony there."

Ben grew impatient, biting his tongue so he would not say anything rude to these senior men. He needed their help, but he sensed the urgency – Cassie needed him –NOW! Meanwhile, Alanja and Bulangi spoke rapid fire Yolngu, a strong awareness of this crisis now coming from them, giving Ben some small relief from his impatience.

"Ben come. We go to Garrawarra house, get Garrawarra, get spears. We find Dumatja – have our own ceremony."

Alanja was happy to let Ben drive his troopy, it gave him a chance to talk with Bulangi about what they had to do. Dumatja had broken Yolngu law, not just white man's law. They knew he must be punished – Yolngu punishment.

Ben was relieved when Garrawarra climbed into the car carrying a handful of spears and a tin of white ochre. Garrawarra was strong and physically he would easily be a match for Dumatja, but a nagging thought crept into Ben's mind as he sped along the dirt track toward that beautiful isolated beach. What about Dumatja's spiritual powers? He was after all a Yolngu witch doctor; could he overcome his three Yolngu friends with his powers? Will he himself be immune? His thoughts raced as quickly as the tree branches swished past the car windows. He had to save her – he had let Laura down and Laura was now dead. *I can't let anything happen to Cassie, not again.* Ben looked back in the mirror and saw the two old men, no longer talking, but looking straight ahead with steel in their eyes. They had taken their shirts off and painted white markings over their faces and bodies. Garrawarra sat quietly beside him, then pointed to a narrow track bearing off the main track. Ben recognised the trees from the time he came here with Karen and the Yolngu women.

"Down there brother. I see car been here not long ago."
Ben did not need to know how Garrawarra knew a car had been there recently, all he could see were ruts in soft sand. He knew their tracking powers. He had been hunting for kangaroo with these men. It was like they had a sixth sense. He had been in awe as one or other of the men described the different animals they knew from the sights, sounds and smells in the bush, none of which had been remotely evident to Ben. He was grateful they would now be able to use these skills to help rescue Cassie. He hoped and prayed quietly that she was unhurt, that she was still alive. The ocean suddenly loomed before them. Garrawarra pointed to another track that led past the large Casuarina tree, the track he hoped with all his heart, would lead them to Cassie.

As they rounded a bend, a white troopy came into view. Ben's stomach was charged with an extra dose of adrenalin, as his body was transformed into an even higher state of alert. He was ready to lay down his life for Cassie if he had to. If he had to, he decided he would fight Dumatja barehanded – there was no other choice, he had to save at least one woman that he loved.

There was no way to creep up and surprise Dumatja, so Ben decided to stop right behind the other troopy and block the only way out. In one movement, he turned the engine off and jumped out of the troopy, Garrawarra and the two elders right behind, resplendent yet fierce in their judicial war paint. Alanja held up a hand and stared hard into the mangrove bushes in front of them. Nobody moved and Ben had the sense to take a back seat – they were in the Yolngu backyard now. He could teach them about building houses, but there was nothing they did not know about this bush. A fallen leaf, a grain of sand out of place, a bird twittering a certain song, all told these men a story – a story that would lead them to Cassie – beautiful Cassie – the woman he loved.

Alanja soon made a move toward the open ocean along the creek bank, beckoning them on with his hand, then fingers to his lips. Each man carried a handful of spears and Ben noticed Garrawarra had a hunting knife in a sheath around his waist. He was careful where he put his feet, trying to step silently, yet the whole time, he wanted to break into a run, his basic instinct was to tear into the bush and frantically make use of the fighting chemicals coursing through his veins. Ben saw the tide rushing in and further panic blanketed his mind. He remembered the choice Dumatja had given Karen. Had Cassie been given the same choice or was she already dead, her body waiting for the crocodile undertaker to remove all evidence of her existence? To remove all evidence that might lock up this crazed Yolngu man forever?

Thoughts continued to torture Ben, as he imagined what Dumatja could have done to Cassie. Finally they emerged at a clearing. Dumatja was before them, ankle deep in rising salty water. He had a knife in his hand and his evil glare was aimed at Alanja. Suddenly he raised his other hand and pointed a bony finger at the old men who were standing proud, spears in hand but pointing at the sky. Dumatja uttered what sounded to Ben like a string of Yolngu curses, venom spat out with every word. Meanwhile, Ben looked across and saw what looked like a person; white shirt in the shadows of a nearby mangrove.

"Cassie – CASSIE!" he yelled before Garrawarra put a hand on Ben's arm and said quietly,

"No Ben. Wait."

Ben was beside himself, he wanted desperately to do something. He wanted to lunge at Dumatja, he wanted to hurt him for hurting Cassie, but most of all, he wanted to go to Cassie, to free her, to console her – to love her, to never let her go.

After Dumatja had finished, Alanja and Bulangi both took turns to speak. Their voices were strong; they sounded like the voices of authority. Ben's impatience was tempered by his trust for these men. Slowly he began to calm inside, as the old men continued speaking. He could see the fire in Dumatja's eyes dying, replaced by uncertainty or even fear. Slowly, the hand holding the knife fell to his side, then his head slumped to his chin. It was then Ben knew Dumatja had been defeated. Alanja and Bulangi stared singing - a mournful Yolngu dirge, haunting and mesmerising. A dirge that made Dumatja walk out of the water and over to them, like a man in a trance. Bulangi and Alanja stepped to either side of Dumatja and the three painted warriors started walking toward the dense bush away from the beach. Garrawarra put his hand on Ben's shoulder and whispered in his ear,

"You go to Cassie now Ben. She okay. You take her back – we come later. We have Yolngu court; now we have Yolngu punishment."

Ben did not have to be asked twice, he burst over to where Cassie was tied, aching to see her, hoping she was unhurt. The tide was already up to her waist; her long cotton skirt floated loosely in the water around her hips. He saw her blue eyes, stained red with tears, then the brown tape over her mouth. He exploded through the water, not even thinking about crocodiles, as he put his hands on Cassie's shoulders and looked down at her. There was no blood, no marks, just streaks where tears had washed away the dust of the bush.

"Oh Cassie –Cassie, you're alright!" He kissed her on the forehead as he slowly started to peel the tape from her mouth.

"Oh Ben, I'm so glad to see you!" Tears flowed down her cheeks as Ben untied the knots that secured her to the giant roots of the mangrove. He worked quickly until she was finally free – finally free to embrace her rescuer, her true white knight who had rescued her. There was desperation in that first hug and the kisses Ben planted on Cassie's head. Now that she was safe and free, Ben allowed himself to cry, their salty tears mingling as their cheeks brushed on the way to a kiss. Cassie was left breathless, her body trembling as she surrendered to Ben's strong arms. They were not even aware of the tide rushing in around them as the joy of this kiss of reunion, this kiss of rescue enveloped them in its power; took them away like whirlpools of the rising tide. At last, Ben came to earth and become conscious of the need to get out of the water. He knew that crocodiles came into the creeks with the tide, but he did not know when.

"Come on Kookaburra, we've got to get out of here. It would be sad if we got away from Dumatja's clutches only to end up as dinner for the croc!" Ben picked her up effortlessly and waded under the mangroves, Cassie's arms around his neck. He gently put her down onto the bank, safe, tears of happiness still falling as they fell into another loving embrace, holding on to each, neither wanting to let go.

"Oh Cassie, I was afraid I'd never see you again."

"You had to see me again Ben, we've got a date to go sailing – remember?" Ben smiled as they released from the embrace. Still holding on to her waist, his eyes were wet as he gazed down tenderly at Cassie.

"You know Rose made me realise something – even before I found out that Dumatja had taken you."

"Rose?"

"Yes. Somehow she made me realise that I can never let you go. She made me admit to myself that I love you Cassie. I love you so much; I never want to leave you. I want to sail with you; I want to drink champagne in the moonlight with you; I, I, want to beat you at arm wrestling!"

"Ha, ha, ha. Ben Brogan, you know what?"

"What?"

"I love you too – and you know what else?"

"What else?"

"If you're a good boy, I might even *let* you beat me at arm wrestling!"

"Oh Cassie. Cassie, will you marry me? I can't offer you much, but I can promise you poetry, adventure and love." Ben faltered at Cassie's silence, "Oh, Cassie, please say yes"."

"Yes Ben. I'll marry you. I don't know about the poetry and after today I'm not sure about the adventure but I'll take all the love you can give."

ABOUT THE AUTHOR

Ed Elgar has broken through the procrastination barrier and finished his first novel. Having worked for 2 years in a wild part of northern Australia, called Arnhem Land, Ed drew upon his own experiences with the Yolngu people, crocodiles and other wild life, in creating the setting for this story.

Having wooed and won the lovely Claire, Ed found himself on his yacht sailing out of San Francisco, destined for Australia. They married in a 12th century church in St Monans, Scotland, and this book was written in a Glasgow cafe while Ed awaited his wedding day.

Ed and Claire now commute between Australia and Scotland, one minute basking and surfing the east coast beaches, the next, climbing Ben Lomond with sandwiches and a thermos of hot tea.

Printed in Great Britain
by Amazon